MA

TERRORISM ON THE NORTH SEA

MARINE A: SBS

TERRORISM ON THE NORTH SEA

Shaun Clarke

First published in Great Britain 1995
22 Books, Invicta House, Sir Thomas Longley Road,
Rochester, Kent

A CIP catalogue record for this book is available from the
British Library

ISBN 1 898125 37 6

10 9 8 7 6 5 4 3 2

Typeset by Hewer Text Composition Services, Edinburgh
Printed in Great Britain by Cox and Wyman Limited, Reading

1

'Is it true the Prime Minister's in the VIP lounge?' McGee asked, wiping his lips with his hand and glancing idly around the crowded heliport lounge.

'That's right,' Tony Masters replied, studying the bottles along the bar. 'Why do you ask? Want to shake the great man's hand?'

McGee laughed sardonically and turned his head to grin at Masters. The Englishman was leaning against the counter, sipping his whisky.

'Ackaye,' McGee said. 'I'd like to shake his hand all right. Then I'd push him off the edge of the drilling floor. For that I'd give my right arm.'

'You're a republican,' Masters said.

'Sure I am,' McGee replied. 'Me and a lot of other right-minded Paddies. Our day will come.'

Masters glanced at the other waiting men with an air of impatience. The heliport lounge was packed and the men on the chairs were surrounded by luggage. Mostly under thirty, they were wearing jeans and anoraks, and were all now hazed in a fog of cigarette smoke. Outside, the weather was filthy, with the airstrip covered in a silvery, wind-blown drizzle. Grounded, the Wessex Mk 3 transport helicopters were parked in well-spaced rows and the drifting clouds cast shadows on their Perspex windows. Masters was annoyed: he wanted to get moving. All the men in the lounge had been there for hours and were no less impatient.

'Look at them,' McGee said softly. 'The scum of the land.'

'Being one of them, you should know,' Masters replied.

The Irishman smiled tightly. His eyes were dark and intense. He had a rough, wind-whipped face, a short, wiry body, and the sort of restless energy that betrays unreleased inner tension.

'I come from them, all right. Sure, I haven't forgotten that. I'm a working-class Paddy and proud of it. But that doesn't mean I'm one of this rubbish.'

'Rubbish?' Glancing around the crowded lounge, Masters saw the unshaven faces of the other men through a veil of cigarette smoke, framed by the windows that looked out on the windy, cloud-darkened heliport. There was a storm over the North Sea, raging around the oil rigs, and the men in the lounge were waiting to board the grounded helicopters. They had been here, in the Bristow Heliport in Aberdeen, for almost five hours.

'Sure they're rubbish,' McGee insisted. 'The dregs

of the working classes. They only work on the rigs because they can't find employment elsewhere.'

'*You* work on the rigs,' Masters said. 'And *I* work on the rigs.'

'Right, Tone. But not because it's the only work we can find. The rigs attract the worthless, the North Sea attracts the debris. Sure, it's a job where you're not asked for your past record or credentials, which is why it appeals to this scum.'

'This is 1982,' Masters said. 'There are approximately *three million* unemployed. The first time since the 1930s. That makes it very easy to be scum.'

After sipping some more beer McGee put his glass down and lit a cigarette with abrupt, nervous movements. Knowing that Masters didn't smoke, he didn't offer him one.

Tony Masters was a bit of a mystery, being a wizard on the oil rigs, seemingly obsessed with work, and rarely discussing his onshore life. McGee was wary of Masters because most of the rig-workers revered him. The Englishman was a tool-pusher, one of the élite of the North Sea: in charge of the drilling, he was tough, efficient and ruthless when it came to hiring and firing. He demanded hard work and obedience from the roughnecks and roustabouts, but he had an almost puritanical sense of justice, which had gained him respect. Too much respect, McGee thought, for a man who had only been on the Frigg Field for six months, reportedly having spent the previous couple of years on the Beryl Field.

'Just think of it,' McGee said. 'Three million unemployed. And that bastard, the Prime Minister, is in the VIP lounge right now, filling his belly.'

'You're not unemployed,' Masters reminded him.

'I'm just a roughneck, Tone. I'm not unemployed, but I could be any day now, just like the others.'

'It's not that bad,' Masters insisted.

'It's that bad and you know it. Sure, with all that unemployment a man can't risk losing his job and the oil companies exploit it to the hilt. We used to have strong unions on the rigs. We still have unions, but they're no longer strong. With unemployment going up by forty thousand a month, the bosses have the whip hand and the unions can't afford to take chances. You're an English tool-pusher. That's a double advantage. You'll have a job as long as there's drilling, but we're not all so lucky.'

If only you knew, Masters thought, resisting the urge to smile.

'As for the oil,' McGee continued, 'it's really in Scottish waters, but the Scots don't get a penny out of it. They're being bled by the fucking Brits, just like the Irish.'

'So what's that got to do with your precious job?' Masters growled. 'You're in charge of every roustabout on your rig. You should be laughing, my friend.'

'Tell us another,' McGee retorted. He took a swig of beer, inhaled on his cigarette and nervously drummed his fingers on the bar. 'The oil beneath the North Sea is estimated at about £2000 million a year. If that revenue went to Scotland, it could meet their national budget *and* give them a healthy balance of payments surplus. I'm amazed the Scottish National Party, who're getting close to a majority, haven't formed their own band of paramilitaries to get that money back from the thieving Brits by taking over the oil rigs. That's what we would do.'

'You back the IRA, then?' Masters asked distractedly, as if making idle conversation.

'No,' McGee said promptly. 'Sure, I'm sympathetic to the cause, but I don't hold with the way they go about it. I'm not into violence.'

'It's comforting to know that,' Masters said sardonically.

'Ackaye, sure it is. They don't trust Irishmen on these rigs. They think all of us back the terrorists, murdering Englishmen in their sleep, so if they need to get rid of the odd worker they always drop the Irish or Scottish first.'

'I don't think that's true,' Masters replied.

'It's true enough,' McGee said.

Masters knew what McGee meant. The oil boom

of the late 1970s had given a lot of men employment, but not all that many had been Scots, let alone Irish. Although the oil was in Scottish waters, ironically the Scots had been forced to take second place to an enormous influx of American, French, Spanish, Norwegian and English workers, with the odd Scot and Irishman thrown in for the sake of appearances. Recently, however, after the Scottish National Party had created a political scandal out of the issue, the oil companies had been bending over backwards to take on more Scottish and Irish workers. In that sense, then, McGee was wrong – or at least out of date.

'Maybe things will change,' Masters said. 'Rumour has it that the real reason the Prime Minister is visiting Bravo 1, in the Forties Field, is for a discussion on the possibility of reducing taxes to encourage the big oil companies to do more drilling. Everyone knows they're deliberately building up huge tax losses in the Middle East and setting the revenue against liability for tax in the UK. They'll carry on like that until the British government reduces tax, and the Prime Minister is obviously aware of the fact.'

'Fuck dealing with them,' McGee retorted. 'The government should nationalize the oilfields and *force* the bastards to drill.'

'They can't do that, McGee. It was the British government that originally granted exploration licences to the oil companies, selling them off by means of an auction with sealed bids. The British sector of the North Sea now belongs legally to them, so if the government stepped in and nationalized, it would lead to an international scandal.'

'Ackaye,' McGee said, glancing around the smoky lounge. 'They're desperate for money, so they sell off the North Sea. Now they're even more desperate and they can't get their hands on the oil. There'll be no sense in this country until Parliament's dismantled and a whole new system introduced. British governments, be they Labour or Conservative, are just capitalist lackeys.'

'You keep talking like that,' Masters said, 'and you *will* lose your job.'

McGee finished his beer. 'Sure, you're not wrong there. A man on the rigs should be tight-lipped. He'll last longer that way.'

Glancing about him, Masters saw the tables piled high with beer cans and crumpled newspapers, the ashtrays overflowing, the cigarette smoke drifting above the heads of the men, whose conversation was a constant, edgy murmuring. Those men worked a fortnight on and a fortnight off. Once on the rigs they would work twelve hours a day, seven days a week, in wet, freezing weather and filth. Since smoking was allowed only when they were off duty, and since the only permissible alcohol was their allowance of two cans of beer a day, they were now doing as much smoking and drinking as possible before going back.

Gazing beyond their heads, out through the plate-glass windows of the lounge, Masters saw the Wessex helicopters parked on the landing pads along the runway, which was also used for light aircraft. Black clouds hung low above them, the rain continued to pour down, and a fierce wind was howling across the airstrip. Out in the North Sea there were Force Nine winds – fifty miles an hour – hurling huge waves against the rigs. The weather ruled the North Sea. It made work costly and dangerous. The men were used to long delays, but that didn't prevent annoyance; and Masters, like the rest of them, was growing edgy.

'I'm going for a piss,' McGee said. 'That should help pass a minute or two. Christ, this business is desperate!'

He slung his rucksack over his shoulder and lumbered off through the milling men, towards the toilet. Masters watched him go, a small smile on his lips, then he surveyed the noisy lounge once more.

Most of the men were quite young. They were a rough-looking bunch. They had come from building sites, from the armed forces or merchant navy, and they were generally the kind of men who, even if married, spent too much time away from home. Work on the rigs, though tough and dangerous, wasn't too highly paid; it appealed to men who could not get work elsewhere or who simply disliked the routine of onshore life. It wasn't a nine-to-five job, you had to serve no apprenticeship, there was no attention paid to previous history or qualifications, and a man with something to hide had to answer few questions.

In a sense they were the last of the brigands. They weren't colourful, but they were distinctive. They were returning, now, after two weeks on shore, where they would have visited families and girlfriends, bought sex in sleazy bedsits, or got drunk in the pubs of Peterhead or Aberdeen. An insular breed, they lived in a small world, working like navvies on the rigs, seldom seeing their relatives, and developing an underplayed camaraderie that gave them moral support.

This mutual support was something that Masters understood, given what he really was and where he came from. He was, in fact, a sergeant with the Royal Marines Special Boat Squadron (SBS), working for the intelligence branch and assigned secretly to the rigs to check out the very real threat of terrorist infiltration, either by Scottish nationalists or by the IRA.

However, his skill as an oil worker was genuine enough. Masters had been a tool-pusher for the oil companies until 1975, when a bad marriage and acrimonious separation had driven him to making his escape by enlisting in the Army, after which he eventually ended up in the Royal Marine Commandos. Soon bored even with that, and wanting to use the knowledge he had picked up on the North Sea rigs, he had applied for the notoriously difficult SBS Potential Recruits' Course (PRC).

After the usual physical and psychological tortures at the Commando Training Centre, Royal Marines, at Lympstone in Devon, he had passed the even more demanding three-week selection test, then undergone a fifteen-week training course in seamanship, navigation, demolition, diving and advanced weapons handling. Among the craft he trained in were paddle-boards, specially-made Klepper Mark 13 collapsibles, Geminis powered by 40bhp outboard motors, and glass-fibre Rigid Raiders powered by 140bhp outboard motors, as used by the specialists of the Royal Marines Rigid Raider Squadron. The main weapons employed by the SBS, he had learned during training, were the US 5.56mm M16 Armalite rifle with M203 grenade-launchers, the 9mm L34A1 Sterling submachine-gun, the standard-issue 9mm Browning High Power handgun, and a variety of plastic explosives. He had also learned to use laser designators, burst-transmission radios, and his extensive survival kit, similar to that used by the SAS.

Having survived the PRC, he had taken an arduous four-week parachute course in Borneo, then been posted to an operational Boat Section, before completing his specialist training at Royal Marines (RM), Poole, Dorset. Accepted by the SBS, he had been allowed to wear the standard uniform of the Royal Marines and the Royal Marine Commando green beret, but with parachuting wings on the right shoulder and the Swimmer Canoeist badge on the right forearm. He had felt proud to do so.

As a member of 41 Commando SBS, he had taken part in exercises in Hong Kong and Borneo, carried out a tour of duty in the Mediterranean with NATO, and endured special Arctic training at Elvergaardsmoen in northern Norway. Promoted to corporal, he had gone undercover for internal security duties in Northern Ireland, sometimes working hand in glove with the SAS and Army Intelligence. Finally, just a few months ago, he had fought in the brief but bloody Falklands war.

After being promoted to sergeant for his leading role in a daring SBS raid designed to set fire to the oil storage tanks in Port Stanley's harbour installations, he had been posted to the intelligence unit of the Portsmouth Group RM, where the work was interesting enough but not very exciting. Luckily, the SBS was then, in strict secrecy, given important responsibilities in the security of Britain's offshore oil and gas rigs. Using his past experience on the rigs as the trump card in his application for a position in North Sea security, he had been accepted and sent to work under cover on Eagle 3, in the Frigg Field, with false papers stating that he had spent the previous two years working on Charlie 2, in the Beryl Field.

His brief was simple: to ensure that no terrorists infiltrated the rig for the purposes of espionage or sabotage. In order to do this, he went back to work as a tool-pusher and was very good at it.

'A man deep in thought,' someone said. 'I *do* like to see that.'

Turning his head, Masters found himself face to face with Robert Barker, who was leaning on the bar at his left shoulder. Blue-eyed and blond, he was wearing a fur-collared pigskin jacket and scruffy blue jeans. Though he looked much younger than his thirty-eight years, he was in charge of security for British United Oil, the conglomerate for which all these men worked. He was also one of the only two men in the North Sea who knew that Masters was SBS.

'Gin and tonic,' he said to the barman. 'And one for my friend here. The best tool-pusher in the business needs his breakfast.'

'Mine was whisky,' Masters informed him.

'I know that,' Barker said. 'And the barman obviously knows your tastes: he's just poured you a large one.'

Masters grinned as the barman set the drinks on the counter. Barker gave him two pounds, waited for his change, then put the coins in his pocket and tried his gin.

'Nice,' he said. '*Very* nice. Day like this, a man needs it.'

'I thought you'd be in with the PM,' Masters said.

'I was,' Barker told him. 'He's having brandy and crisps. The brandy's a sign that he's an ambitious Prime Minister; the crisps mean he's still one of the lads. It's what's known as good politics.'

Masters grinned again. 'I'm surprised you're not still in there. You're supposed to be our top security man.'

'How can I protect him? He's already surrounded by bodyguards and military police. If they can't do the job, no one can. Anyway, my real job is to protect the Forties Field. Our esteemed PM is spending two days and one night on Bravo 1 and I've had that platform checked from top to bottom. I also have men all over the place.' He sipped his drink. 'I believe you won't be joining us this time.'

'No,' said Masters. 'I'm flying out to Eagle 3 in the Frigg Field to start closing it down. We'll soon be towing it away to another site.'

'Frigg's dried out?'

'Yeah. It was the most used field during the boom years and now the oil's all gone.'

'I would have come across sooner,' Barker said,

abruptly changing the subject, 'but I didn't want to interrupt your conversation with that nice man, McGee.'

'He's a real pain in the arse. But he happens to be a good worker.'

'He's a troublemaker. He backs the unions to the hilt. Two years ago, when we were having all those strikes, McGee was up to his neck in it.'

'So he's a union man. A *lot* of our men are in the union. I don't give a toss as long as they get on with their work. McGee's all right. He's just a bit obsessed. If he catches you at the bar, he's a pain, but he does do his work.'

Barker sighed. 'I suppose you're right. I just can't stand the bastard.'

Masters smiled consolingly. 'You don't have to work with the bastard – and neither do I.'

'I guess that's right,' Barker said.

They touched glasses and drank, then glanced around the crowded lounge bar. To the casual observer the men would have looked like a single group, but the more experienced eye saw segregation. The rig workers, who felt divorced from the outer world, were also divorced from one another by the singular hierarchy of the oilfields. Packed together in the smoky lounge, they had instinctively moved into their own, very separate groups.

The majority were roustabouts, general labourers who worked on the lower decks of the rigs, unloading the supply boats and moving the machinery or steel pipes in and out of the storage space and up to the drilling floor. They did this and every other unskilled job and in general were the lowest-paid men on the rigs.

The second largest group were the roughnecks, men who worked on the drilling floor, usually around the roaring shaft, changing the bits that had broken on rocks 11,000 feet beneath the ocean bed and extending the drills by adding lengths of heavy steel piping. It was skilled, exhausting, dangerous work and the roughnecks were therefore paid more than the roustabouts.

These two very different groups formed the backbone of the rigs, but their jobs usually kept them apart. Working seven days a week, twelve hours a day, they weren't given enough spare time to strike up close friendships with anyone outside their immediate environment.

Even more remote were the key men, the tool-pushers, who kept a tight rein on the roustabouts and roughnecks and were directly responsible only to company supervisors. The tool-pushers were a breed apart; they had total authority over the other men. If their status could be rivalled, only the divers could come close – not because they had authority, but because their high fatality rate placed them near the top of the wage structure. The divers were the most insular; their odd way of life made them so.

During their time on the rigs they would either be diving or suffering the harrowing isolation of decompression. It was a bizarre way of life – like that of an astronaut. Either under the sea or in a decompression chamber, enduring the danger and monotony of relentless saturation diving, they would not be in physical touch with their fellow human beings for the whole of their two weeks on board. So they were strangers, hardly known to the other men; and in this lounge, in the grey haze of cigarette smoke, they remained a group well apart.

Listening to the murmuring, the sudden outbursts of laughter, the rattling of beer cans and scuffling of restless feet, Masters felt that he had truly come home. The fragments of conversation he overheard were a mixture of the profane and the technological, bringing back the feel and taste of a world that was as far removed from the normal world as was the moon from the earth.

'. . . still drilling for Complex, but expect to complete the current and final hole shortly. Then the rig'll be towed to Hamburg for the demob of diving equipment and a lengthy refit. Then God knows where else . . .'

'. . . "rig workers' widows", they call them. They say they never see their men. The divorce rate's going up and there's far too much booze going down. That's why *my* marriage is doomed . . .'

'. . . definitely a hell of an improvement. Unscrambled speech facilities from the diver back to the bellman; processed speech side-tone speaker for clear speech between diver and bellman; diver tape connections plus tape connections for playback in all chambers; and a good ten hours' life in the power pack . . .'

'. . . it can't go on much longer. She keeps coming to the boarding house. Says I picked her up in the Granada in Peterhead and then got her pregnant. Lying cow! I don't even know her name . . .'

'. . . wind a hundred and fucking thirty, waves ninety foot high. Fucking tanker crashed into the platform and all hell broke loose. Five of the crew were killed, a two-mile slick on the sea, then the bloody well-head exploded and I blacked out and woke up in the knacker's yard. What the fuck am I doing here?'

'. . . Sidko 803 just returned to Rover Oil after drilling a well for BP. Now on permanent contract to Rover since BP no longer seem interested in the rig. Meanwhile, Beta 45 is in the Netherlands having its Comex 1000 system replaced and will soon be operating for . . .'

'. . . a hell of a storm. Dumb bastard fell down the moonpool. Another hit in the face with a bolt from the shaft and a load fell on the crane-driver's cab. They tried to burn through the metal. The storm blew up again. The crane broke loose and was swept into the sea. Four degrees in there, it was . . .'

'. . . I can't go home again. It's all over for good this time. She said it was the North Sea or her, so I picked the North Sea . . .'

Masters listened to the words and heard a familiar refrain. It made him think of the Royal Marine Commandos, the weapons and the boats, the exercises and the undercover activities in Belfast. It was a world in which men without women looked to hard work for comfort. It was an unstated machismo code, removing a man from the normal, and it gave rise to a feeling of freedom that was not quite definable. The North Sea held that attraction. The oil rigs were a world apart. They encouraged fierce competition and a chauvinistic pride that had long since disappeared from onshore life. Masters liked this male world, with its constant action. He'd been married, but was divorced three years later because he couldn't stay at home for long. Masters wanted his freedom, as did a lot of the rig workers. The men who drilled the North Sea, who braved the wind and freezing rain, the dizzying heights, the constant danger, were pioneers of the most ordinary cut, but they *did* stand apart.

'I think the Prime Minister's leaving,' Barker said. 'Let's take a look.'

Glancing up, Masters saw the other men turning instinctively toward the windows that overlooked the landing pads. Following Barker, he pushed through to the front and looked out at the silent helicopters. The rain was still pouring. The wind blew it across the airstrip. The sky was dark and the greyness was foreboding, the view chilly and desolate.

Farther along the airstrip, military policemen were emerging from the sandbagged entrance to the VIP lounge. Bulky in boots and helmets, carrying 9mm Sterling Light Automatic Rifles, they emerged in two lines that formed a grim, protective path for the Prime Minister. Beyond them were two aircraft hangars, rain pouring down their walls; on top of the hangars were more Army marksmen, scanning the heliport.

The Prime Minister emerged, wearing a black overcoat. A man in a dark-grey suit was holding an umbrella over his head while other men in similar suits poured out around him, their hands under their jackets, resting on their Brownings.

Masters watched them carefully. The whole scene was depressing. The men moving towards the airstrip through the rain and howling wind looked like Mafia hit men. There was no ceremony here; simply a watchful, nervous advance. The MPs, holding their sub-machine-guns at the ready, fanned out towards the nearest Wessex while the Prime Minister and his entourage hurried between them, all with heads bowed.

'It's still filthy weather,' Barker said. 'That's a pretty strong wind out there.'

'It must be dying,' Masters replied. 'Almost certainly it's passed over the rigs. They wouldn't let the PM take off otherwise. We'll probably all take off soon.'

'A lot of armour,' Barker observed. 'I never thought I'd see the day. There are enough weapons and ammunition in this heliport to start a bloody war.'

'He needs it,' Masters said. 'The assassination list is growing. It's even been rumoured that a bomb was found in the House of Commons. This whole country's a war zone.'

'Happy days,' Barker said.

Masters looked at the distant hangars and saw the glint of binoculars, the barrel of a machine-gun moving from side to side in a slow, searching motion. Smiling tightly, shaking his head in disbelief, he returned his thoughtful gaze to the helicopters. The Prime Minister was entering the nearest one in the row, being helped up by a bodyguard. He disappeared inside, and his entourage followed him. The military police formed a cordon around the chopper as it roared into life. The rotor blades whipped up the wind as they blurred and merged into a single line. The military police stood beneath them with their uniforms flapping furiously and their weapons together covering every direction.

The Wessex carrying the Prime Minister roared louder, shook and rose a little, turned towards the east, climbed higher and disappeared through the low clouds.

The men around Masters relaxed, then returned to their chairs. Their conversation became louder and more ebullient, as if a crisis had passed. Masters remained at the window, still standing beside Barker. McGee came up to stand between them and gaze out at the cloudy grey sky.

'He's left,' Masters said.

'Sure, I saw that,' McGee said. 'Now maybe we can all get out of here and back to work.'

'It won't be long,' Masters said.

2

The Prime Minister gazed through the window of the helicopter and saw, far below him, through the haze of thinning cloud, the choppy grey desolation of the North Sea. It made him shiver. He felt cold and slightly unreal. The sea stretched out as far as the eye could see and then was lost in drifting clouds.

'It looks terribly cold down there,' he said. 'I would not like to work there.'

'No, Prime Minister,' replied the Under-Secretary of the Department of Energy. 'Neither would I.'

The PM chuckled and gave a fleeting, sardonic smile. He had a florid, well-fleshed, stubborn face with cold blue eyes and grey hair. The Under-Secretary, beside him, had the appearance of a young executive; unlike the PM he had not come up the hard way and the differences between them often showed. Now the PM sighed, keeping his gaze on the North Sea, and his large body shifted uneasily as the clouds drifted past him.

'Well,' he said, 'it's not a job for the likes of me.

It's a job for the sort of man my father was. It must be a rough life.'

Opening his briefcase, the Under-Secretary glanced up in surprise. His accent, unlike the PM's, was public-school.

'You sound almost nostalgic, Prime Minister. That world died a long time ago.'

'Did it? I'm not so sure of that. Those lads aren't paid as much as they're worth and both of us know it.'

'I thought they were paid quite well.'

'You think the miners get paid well?'

'Don't they?'

'The pay's good, but it's not enough for what we ask them to do. And I believe the North Sea's worse than the mines. The fatality rate is high. In fact, according to my reports, the chances of death are ten times as great as in mining.'

'And fifty times as great as in general industry, Prime Minister.'

'Precisely.'

The PM sounded annoyed and the Under-Secretary, smiling slightly, removed some papers from his briefcase. The PM turned his head, saw the papers, and returned his gaze to the sea below.

'Where are the guards?' he asked.

'Up at the front.'

'SAS?'

'SBS – Special Boat Squadron.'

'In case we go down?'

'Yes, Prime Minister.'

The PM grinned sardonically, still studying the restless sea a long way below him. 'I've got to stay on the rig until tomorrow night?'

'Yes, Prime Minister.'

'I hope I'm not seasick.'

'You won't be. You'll be staying on the concrete platform, not on a rig.'

'I thought they were *all* rigs.'

'No, they're not. It's the rig that makes one seasick. A rig is used for test drilling – to check if there's oil in a given spot. Most of the rigs are semi-submersible, with the greater portion of their weight below water, usually in the shape of enormous pontoons and held down by fourteen-ton anchors. They are, in a sense, like floating factories and they *do* pitch and sway just like ships. But the platforms are different. Once a rig finds an oilfield, a platform is sent out to replace it. The rig drills to find oil; the platform houses the production machinery when they actually start bringing the oil up. Made of concrete, the platform's main deck is about the size of Trafalgar Square, and its legs are planted firmly on the seabed. It's more an island than a mere floating factory and it probably doesn't sway as much as high-rise flats. We're going to the new Forties Field platform, the largest in the North Sea. All the oil from the other fields now flows through the Forties and goes back through a single pipeline to Peterhead.' The Under-Secretary paused to give the Prime Minister time to take in this information. 'This platform is really huge. It's almost a self-contained refinery. We won't feel a tremor and I really don't think you'll be seasick.'

The PM nodded, his gaze still fixed on the grey sheet of cold, deadly water. The Wessex roared and shuddered. There was still a wind outside. Inside there were forty-four seats with not one of them vacant. The PM sighed, feeling tired and edgy. The last three years had been terrible, a general election was being demanded, and the importance of this trip weighed heavily upon him, making him nervous.

'What do you think?' he asked abruptly.

'About the oil companies?'

'Yes.'

'I think we'll have to tread with care. They're not easy to deal with.'

'No. They're not easy to deal with. I sometimes wonder who really runs the country – us or the conglomerates.'

The Under-Secretary smiled, knowing what the PM meant. He gazed at the reports in his hand but learnt little from them.

'They're a problem,' he agreed. 'They're almost beyond jurisdiction. We have to think of the voters, British interests, the long term, but the conglomerates are nearly all multinational and don't recognize boundaries. They're not tied to any single country. They simply trade among themselves. If they have a problem with one country, they move their assets to another and there's always one that will offer a tax haven. That's why we're in trouble. They're not willing to pay our taxes. Now they've practically stopped work in the North Sea and instead have turned their attention to the Middle East, where they enjoy tax-free profits beyond belief.'

'Those are *British* companies.'

'No, Prime Minister, they're not. They're multinationals with their roots overseas; the so-called British companies are merely their subsidiaries. As for the *British* companies, they're simply sitting on their oil, claiming they can't afford to invest any more and patiently waiting for us to give in and lower the current oil tax.'

'Bastards,' the Prime Minister said flatly.

'Exactly,' the Under-Secretary said. 'But we no longer have a choice; we have to negotiate with them.'

The PM shuddered again. He had been feeling older recently. He sometimes felt that he had been at this game too long; that he could no longer handle it. There were no simple answers, the ground was shifting all the time, and the politician had to share all his decisions with the unions and businessmen.

Who indeed ran the country? It was a question he often asked himself. There were forces beyond the reach of mere governments that could make and break policies. The government was no more than a mouthpiece, an imperfect focus for public attention. Behind the scenes, in private boardrooms and in far-away continents, the real decision-makers ruled the world.

'How far out is the Forties Field?' he asked, keen to change the subject.

'Just over a hundred miles.'

'It's not near Shetland, then?'

'No. Frigg and Beryl are near Shetland; about halfway between Shetland and Norway.'

'Still, it'll be cold there.'

'Yes, Prime Minister.'

'I hope they don't get any gales.'

'Unfortunately, they get a lot. They even get gales in summer. Work on the rigs is totally subject to weather and the North Sea is terrible in that respect. It makes things costly, destroying rigs, wrecking schedules. Supply boats often toss at anchor for days, sometimes weeks, just waiting until unloading can start. They often can't tow rigs away, men are frequently swept overboard, and rigs are sometimes blown off their sites and have to be towed back. So yes, they get gales all right.'

The PM shifted uneasily in the seat and massaged his ruddy chin with his right hand.

'The Scots won't like it,' he said, returning to the first, uncomfortable subject. 'They'll say we're giving their oil away to make a quick profit. They're getting close to a majority, they're demanding independence, and they'll want the oil to be there when they get it.'

'*If* they get it, Prime Minister.'

'I don't think we can discount the possibility, though it may take a long time. Meanwhile, we've the Irish to contend with. What about them?'

'You mean their threats against the oil rigs?'

'Precisely.'

'The rumours that the IRA are planning to hijack the rigs and hold the British government to ransom remain just that: rumours. So far we have no cause to think otherwise.'

'But what if they *did* do what they threatened and captured the oil rigs? How would that effect us?'

'Frankly, Prime Minister, it would be a catastrophe. With the economy on the verge of collapse, only North Sea oil revenue can possibly save it. The Irish Troubles continue, our unemployment is shockingly high, overseas investors are pulling out with increasing frequency, and the possibility of economic collapse has become public knowledge. That's why we so desperately need the oil revenue: it's all we have left. If the rigs were to be taken over or, even worse, destroyed, our economy would collapse overnight.'

'Wonderful,' the PM said drily. 'I trust we've taken the necessary safeguards.'

'Yes, Prime Minister. Naturally. There's at least one top security man on every rig and platform. Each rig and platform also has an SBS intelligence man operating under cover as a rig worker. On shore, both the SBS and the SAS are on constant alert, ready to be flown in at thirty minutes' notice. Even if these measures fail and one of the rigs or platforms is somehow captured, it will be an isolated incident that can't affect the other rigs and platforms. By this I mean that no group can steal the entire oilfield network, which is what they'd have to do in order to hold us to ransom. For instance, if a bunch of terrorists capture a rig, we'll simply leave them there until they give in, letting them starve to death if necessary. Meanwhile the other rigs, being many, sometimes hundreds, of miles apart, will keep operating. In other words, individual rigs or platforms may be endangered, but the oilfields are safe.'

'Let's hope so,' the PM said.

'We're going down,' the Under-Secretary noted. 'We must have reached the Forties.'

Glancing out through the window, the PM saw the bleak, wind-whipped sea. There was a derrick on a platform far below, looking terribly desolate. Then the helicopter dropped lower. He saw a second rig, then a third. One of the rigs was burning off its waste gas and the smoke billowed sideways. The helicopter dropped lower. The rigs started looking bigger. He saw a square-shaped concrete platform with huge legs and crossbeams and a couple of frail-looking derricks. The platform didn't move as the sea poured between its legs. The helicopter continued its descent, and the platform grew wider and taller, taking on shape and detail.

It was huge, like a giant Meccano set. The towering derricks and cranes, steel catwalks and metal tanks, piles of crates and a plethora of prefabricated buildings impressed the PM; he felt an unaccustomed, childlike awe. The helicopter dropped lower, to below the tallest derrick . . . and then suddenly the massive platform was spread out to his right like some monolith from an unknown world.

The legs were incredibly wide and webbed with thick steel beams. The sea surged up to smash against the legs, then fell back and rushed in again. The PM held his breath. He saw the helicopter pad. Circled in blue and white, it was on the edge of the platform, and loomed nearly 200 feet above the sea, just above the main deck. The helicopter dropped towards it. The steel-webbed derricks grew taller. The PM glanced up, but he couldn't see the tops of the derricks, so he looked down again. The landing pad rushed up towards him with the sea far below it. The monstrous steel maze swung around him in a grey haze, then suddenly it was towering above him, reaching up to the stormy sky.

The PM licked his lips. The helicopter roared even louder. It bumped on to the landing pad and bounced a few times, then finally came to a shuddering rest. Its engine died and the spinning rotor blades separated. Staring out in a daze, the PM saw a huge factory where men hung from metal girders, clambered up swaying ladders, crossed catwalks swept by spray, crawled along lengths of steel pipes that swayed dangerously above the roaring waves. Then the PM looked down. He saw the sea far below. An enormous concrete leg plunged towards it and made him feel dizzy.

'Home and dry,' someone said cheerily.

3

The rotors of the Wessex were still spinning when Tony Masters jumped out of the helicopter and stood on the landing pad of Eagle 3, Frigg Field. The wind whipped his face and he breathed the fresh, freezing sea air. When a man in red overalls waved at him, he grinned and waved back. The chopper's engine tapered off and the rotors finally stopped spinning. Two men in yellow overalls placed blocks around the wheels as the pilot jumped down behind Masters. The pilot combed his brown hair, chewed gum and grinned at nothing in particular as he gazed about him.

Masters looked at the floating factory that soared up to the grey sky and heard the savage roaring of the drilling shaft. Too big to be imagined, the rig never failed to impress him. It was a factory built for giants and the men were like ants beneath the huge structures. They were working on the muddy deck, which was a maze of cranes and loading bays, countless lamps and antennae, three-ton pipes and Portakabins. Though a quarter of a mile wide, the deck rose and fell constantly. Beneath it there were two other floors; beneath those, the massive legs.

'Shall I get them out?' the pilot, Jack Schulman, asked.

Masters nodded and glanced down at the sea way below him. It was grey and quite rough, washing around the pontoon legs, stretching out to the distant horizon, now obscured in a dismal haze. This was a semi-submersible rig. It had four main pontoon legs, thirty feet wide and nearly three hundred feet long, which plunged eighty feet beneath the sea to the massive pontoons. The pontoon legs were hollow and webbed with steel ladders. The pontoons themselves were filled with water and attached to the seabed with huge anchor chains.

'All right!' Schulman bawled. 'Shake your asses!'

Glancing over his shoulder, Masters saw the first of the replacement crew clambering down out of the Wessex. Beyond the helicopter, stretching out to the horizon, was the featureless grey mass of the North Sea. The chopper seemed to rise and fall. The deck was swaying to and fro. The men were clambering down and piling up their luggage on the vibrating landing pad. In fact, the whole rig was vibrating. The central shaft continued roaring. The jib of a distant crane swung out over the sea and its thick chain rattled over the side.

Masters shivered and clapped his hands. The

wind was constant and always icy. Eagle 3 was two hundred miles north of Aberdeen, halfway between the Shetlands and Norway. Originally its oil had been piped down through Beryl to the Orkneys, but threats from the IRA had put a stop to that and now it went on through Beryl to the Forties Field, where about now the Prime Minister would be landing.

'OK,' Masters said to the men grouped around the Wessex. 'Sort out your gear, then follow that man in yellow overalls – that's Jim Webb, by the way – down to your quarters. Let me remind you new men to watch your step. Don't trip on anything, don't fall off the edge, and *don't* let the wind blow you away.' Some of the men laughed at that, but they stopped when Masters stared coldly at them. 'I'm not kidding,' he said. 'These rigs are extremely dangerous. The decks are slippery with mud and oil, machinery often breaks loose, and the wind can unexpectedly turn fierce and blow men off the catwalks. The sea's two hundred feet below. The water temperature's five degrees Celsius. So if you don't break your neck when you fall, you'll freeze to death in minutes. OK, let's get moving.'

The men sorted out their gear and followed Jim Webb to the steps that led down from the landing pad to the deck below. The deck was swaying, dipping towards the sea and back up, the waves growling and smashing against the pontoon legs and sending spray fanning into the air. Masters looked at the derrick. Grey clouds drifted above it. It was a hundred and fifty feet tall, its tapering legs webbed with steel, and its square base rested firmly on the roof of the semi-enclosed drilling deck. The drill shaft was rotating, making a Godalmighty roaring. Around the shaft, on the edge of the immense deck, cranes shrieked and turned back and forth.

'You gonna sign for this lot, Masters?'

Schulman, chewing gum, was standing beside the tool-pusher and holding out the passenger list. When Masters signed it, Schulman winked and spat out his gum. He put his hand in his pocket, pulled out another stick, unwrapped it, slid it between his teeth and started chewing again.

'Why did you bring those new kids?' he asked. 'I heard this rig's closing down.'

'It is. We're towing it away next week. The work on board will be light and we can teach the new ones easier that way.'

'Hi-ho,' Schulman said in his broad Montana accent. 'I have another load to go back. What time are they leaving?'

'About an hour,' Masters told him. 'One, maybe two. I've got to check the new ones in before I can check out the old. So just hang on to your balls and we'll get there.'

'Fireball Masters,' Schulman said. 'Read you

loud and clear, chief.' He grinned as he chewed. After glancing at the stormy sea far below, he zipped up his bright-red flying jacket. 'A nice place to work,' he said, shivering in the wind. 'It sure beats air-conditioning.'

Masters grinned at him. 'You're getting soft, Jack. It's the curse of being born an American; your bones have gone soft.'

'Oh, yeah,' Schulman replied. 'Don't I know it? Now you, Masters, you're just a goddamn monster. You've got no sensitivity.'

'I eat a healthy breakfast,' Masters said. 'I try not to masturbate. I'm a clean-living, all-British lad, and I work for my tuppence.'

'How'd you get to be a tool-pusher?'

'I worked for my tuppence.'

'Come *on*, Tone! Most of the tool-pushers are American, so how did you get the job?'

'I honestly can't remember.'

'Bullshit! You're snowing me. Anyway, my friend, you sure climbed fast. You must've been pretty good. The oil companies don't normally think so highly of Limey rig workers. Yeah, you must've been sharp.'

'Thank you, Jack, for those kind words.'

The pilot grinned. 'You going down now?'

'Yeah.'

'I'll come down for a beer.'

Masters picked up his rucksack and they both

walked away from the helicopter. Located above the main deck, the landing pad was joined to it by a steep catwalk. Beneath the catwalk was nothing but a dizzying plunge to the water. Stopping halfway across, Masters looked out over the sea. On the horizon was a rig, barely distinguishable except for the dark smoke from waste gas coiling skyward. Masters looked down and saw the huge, slanting leg. Hollow supports, a yard thick, formed a web beneath the decks and angled down about a hundred and forty feet to join the pontoon legs. The sea smashed against the legs, making a hollow drumming sound. The shifting shadow of the rig turned the grey water black and made it look even more frightening.

'Hey, Masters, what the fuck are you doing? Planning a swim?'

Already on the deck, Schulman was waving up at Masters. He looked small and he was shouting against the noise as the wind beat at him. Masters waved and clambered down, keeping his hand on the railing. He stepped on to the deck with great care, seeing patches of oil and mud.

'These rigs are fucking filthy, man,' Schulman said. 'I don't know how you can work here.'

They started across the open deck. The oil and mud had made it slippery. From the centre of the deck, to their right, came the roar of the drilling room. They passed stacks of iron piping, then went under a raised crane which was rumbling fifty feet above their heads on a broad, round steel base. Masters stopped to glance up. The crane was picking up some large wooden crates with men standing on top of them and holding on to the thick chain of the jib. The crane whined and turned around, swinging the men out on the crates. They swung out beyond the deck, high above the sea, shouting instructions as the crates were lowered to the supply boat below.

'Goddamn roustabouts,' Schulman growled.

'Yeah,' replied Masters. 'They're obviously taking off the heavier equipment before the tow starts.'

They started walking again. When a yellow fork-lift trundled past them, the driver shouted a greeting and waved at Masters. Masters waved back as he passed some cursing roustabouts. They were leaning on a spanner that was bigger than a man, straining to disconnect two massive pipes, forty-five feet long and each weighing three tons. The men cursed and strained. The wind lashed across the deck, which constantly vibrated, swayed from side to side, and gave off an insane metallic shrieking and the roar of the drilling shaft. The sea smashed relentlessly against the hollow pontoon legs and made them reverberate.

Schulman reached one of the modules, opened the door and bowed to Masters. The tool-pusher grinned and stepped in, followed by the American. They heard a deep, muffled rumbling.

'Just show me the bar,' Schulman said. 'I could do with a drink.'

Masters unzipped his jacket. 'No spirits allowed,' he said. 'We *do* permit two cans of beer a day. You can take it or leave it.'

Schulman grinned and chewed his gum. 'Fucking hot in here. Yeah, I'll take you up on that offer. It's the beer I came down for.'

They were in a narrow, low-ceilinged, brightly lit corridor. It was just like a ship, with many steps, steel doors, and passages leading off in several directions. It was one of the many prefabricated buildings known as modules. Erected after the rig had been towed to its site, they could easily be dismantled and offloaded.

'It's a morgue,' Schulman said.

'The living quarters and operations rooms,' Masters informed him.

'Christ, I feel buried here.'

Masters led the pilot along the corridor, turned the corner at the end, then went along another corridor, its steel walls painted white, and disappeared through an open door. Schulman followed him into a cluttered office module. It had a single porthole, through which the hazy horizon could be seen. Another white-painted wall was occupied by a large map of the North Sea, while a third was covered with various nautical charts and graphs. A heavy, suntanned man was sitting behind the desk. Schulman recognized a redneck when he saw one and knew this Yank was a redneck.

'How are you, Tone?' the man drawled. 'You bin gettin' your rocks off?'

'Dipped it once or twice,' Masters replied. 'Academic interest, mainly.'

'Jesus,' the redneck said, 'you goddamn Brits. Always quick with the come-back.' He scratched his nose and stared at Schulman. 'Who the hell's that?' he asked Masters. 'Looks like Jack Nicholson.'

'First name's right,' Schulman informed him. 'Jack Schulman. I'm the pilot who's taking your old crew back. When do we leave?'

The man yawned and stretched. After rubbing his face with his hands, he stood up and gazed through the porthole.

'They're already waiting in the canteen,' he said. 'They've been cleared to leave.'

'Any problems in my absence?' Masters asked.

'No problems. Apart from the fact that most Brits are lazy cunts, it's all been hunky-dory on Eagle 3.' Grinning, the redneck turned back to face Masters. He was wearing grey trousers and a shirt that advertised Twentieth Century Oil. 'We're offloading the heavy gear and extracting the blow-back preventer. We'll soon be putting the locks on the cranes and then it's all set to go. It'll look like a ghost ship.'

He yawned again and rubbed his eyes. Schulman noticed that his shoes were covered in oil and a thin, slimy mud.

'Are you going back?' Masters asked him.

'Yeah, I'm goin' back. I'm having two weeks onshore and then I'm taking over a rig in the Forties.'

'There'll be a lot of work there shortly.'

'There hasn't been in the past. That fucking government of yours has killed it off and we're not playing ball.'

'That's going to change,' Masters informed him. 'The Prime Minister's there right now. I think he's going to reduce the oil tax. If he does, we'll start drilling.'

'I hope so,' the redneck drawled. 'I sure as hell hope so. I don't want to be pensioned off.' He grinned again at Masters. 'So,' he said, 'I better get ready to leave. Go and get your new boys organized – and send mine up to the chopper.'

Masters and Schulman left the cabin, and made their way down a flight of steel stairs and into the canteen. It was a functional, brightly lit room with white tables and blue-leatherette chairs. The replacement crew were eating T-bone steaks with chips and mushrooms. The departing crew were drinking at the bar. Since hard liquor wasn't allowed on the rigs, they were all guzzling beer.

'Hey, Masters!' one of them shouted across the room. 'When the fuck are we leaving?'

'Leaving?' Masters replied dourly. 'You want to leave? I just don't understand that.'

Most of the men laughed. 'I want the night-life of Aberdeen,' one of them said. 'I'm in need of a quick thrill.' More laughter followed. 'Two weeks on shore, that's all,' someone else said. 'What's the delay?'

Masters grinned and put his hands up as if holding them at bay. 'Take it easy,' he said. 'The chopper's being refuelled right now and when that's done you can go.' The men at the bar cheered. 'OK,' Masters said when the cheering had died away. 'I want you to wait in the recreation room. You can take your beer with you. We'll call you when we're ready to leave. That's it. On your way.'

The men cheered again, traded ribald remarks, slapped each other on the back, then picked up their luggage and filed out of the canteen.

'Right,' Masters said, remaining standing to address the men still at the tables, 'put your knives and forks down and listen. You regular crew members know what I'm going to say, but you'll just have to bear with me. You new men, please note these facts. Most of you have probably worked in a factory before and an oil rig resembles a factory. But that resemblance is deceptive. An oil rig is very different. For one thing, it floats. That means it's always rolling. The decks are slippery and it's easy to lose your footing and slide right off the edge. It's a two-hundred-foot drop. If you survive the fall, you won't survive the sea, so try not to fall. A rig is also exposed. An average North Sea wind can be something like fifty miles an hour and it often reaches a hundred and sometimes a hundred and fifty. We get waves the size of your average office block. They wreck machinery and swallow men. Even a modest gale can cause chains to snap and then all hell breaks loose. Watch out for flying bolts. Beware of sliding equipment. It's easy to get crushed between crates when they slide on the decks. And be careful on the catwalks. Keep your hands on the railings. When a man gets too cocky he gets careless and that's something he can't afford. Men have been swept off the catwalks. They've fallen down the moonpool. They've been hit by flying bolts, crushed between machines, and killed by equipment falling from cranes or the platforms above them. Believe me, all this happens.'

The men, he noticed, were all listening carefully, impressed by the sound of his voice and his air of authority. He had picked up this skill in the SBS and he was now grateful for it.

'About your work,' he continued. 'It's two weeks on and two weeks off. What you do on shore is your own business, but on the rig you'll obey all the rules. Work on the rig goes on all around the clock in two shifts. You work twelve hours a day, seven days a week. You sleep four to a room, but since you all work in shifts, there'll only be two of you sleeping at any one time. Work is hard on the rigs and you'll find that you need your sleep, so you won't want to be disturbed by the other two men. Bear this in mind if you have to go to your room, and try not to disturb the ones sleeping. If you do and a man complains you'll be dismissed and that's that. You have a recreation room with a film on every evening. You're only allowed to smoke in off-duty space and off-duty time; and the only alcohol permitted is your free allowance of two cans of beer a day. Anyone caught breaking these rules will be flown back on the next available chopper with no chance to appeal.'

Masters stared at the new intake, his face firm and uncompromising, his hands on his hips, his long legs outstretched.

'Another point to remember,' he continued. 'Most of these rigs are hired from drilling companies and are indirectly under their supervision. Now although you men are employed by the oil company, you'll find yourselves dealing with men employed by the drilling company, a geological company, repair and maintenance companies, and a catering company. Don't mess with any of these people. Avoid all disputes with them. If you've any complaints go direct to your foreman and let him investigate the matter. Anyone breaking this rule, whether for good reasons or bad, will end up on the first chopper back to Aberdeen.'

He turned to the wall behind him and picked up the telephone. 'Hello, Segal? This is Masters. Get yourself down to the canteen. I've got some new men here.' He put the receiver back on its hook and then turned to the men again. 'You'll find a guide to the rig on your beds. Study it carefully, have a good look around, then report to the foreman named at the top of the guide. His location will be marked on the scale drawing. He'll tell you when and where you'll be starting. Once you've started, make sure you do what you're told and don't piss around. If you cause any trouble, you'll be dismissed – and I'm notoriously deaf to excuses.'

A man entered the canteen. He was wearing overalls and boots, his brown hair was dishevelled, and he was covered from top to bottom in mud and oil. He grinned and nodded at Masters, waving a grimy hand, then glanced at the new men.

'I've just completed the briefing,' Masters said, 'so you can show them down to their quarters, then tell Delaney you've got them.'

'Right, chief,' the man said.

The men were led out of the canteen and Masters and Schulman went to the bar. Masters asked for two beers, snapped the lids on both cans, then pushed one of the cans across to the American.

'There,' he said, 'have some vitamins.'

Schulman rolled his eyes and drank some beer. He wiped his lips with the back of his left hand and grunted with pleasure.

'That was a pretty good speech, Tone,' he said. 'I could feel my flesh creeping.'

Masters grinned. 'I'm glad it got through to *someone*. It's a pity you can't practise what I preach. Why not stay for a fortnight?'

'No thanks, man. I feel safer in my chopper. The only thing you've got to offer is beer and that ain't enough.'

'I'd keep you busy,' Masters promised.

'I bet you would,' Schulman replied. 'You'd run my ass ragged and then send me back home in a pine box. Thanks, but no thanks.'

Masters drank some more beer, then glanced around the almost empty canteen. It wasn't very different from the canteens in the various SBS bases he had passed through. That was why he felt so at home.

'What about those guys I'm taking back?' Schulman asked. 'Do I go get them now?'

'No, not yet. I've got to check a few things first. Once the men know they're shore-bound they're inclined to get careless and leave cock-ups that can cause a lot of damage. I want a quick look round first. I want to check that none of the bastards have fouled up in their urge to take off.'

'And what if someone has?'

'Then you'll be taking him back to Aberdeen and leaving him there. I won't want him back.'

'You're a tough nut, Tone.'

'Which is why your American friends appreciate me. Now drink up and let's go.'

They finished their drinks and left the canteen, with Masters leading the way down more steel steps and along narrow corridors, passing storerooms, administration modules, living accommodation and the radio shack. All the corridors were brightly lit, all the ceilings were low, and the many portholes overlooked the heaving sea and its murky horizon. There was a constant bass rumbling that grew louder as they descended more steps. Suddenly it turned into a shocking roar that shattered the senses.

They were on the drilling floor. A massive derrick towered above them. The drilling floor was walled in, but it was open to the sky, and there was a large, square-shaped hole in the deck: the 'moonpool'. The sea was two hundred feet below it, and enormous lengths of piping plunged down through the hole over twice that distance to the seabed. The central shaft was roaring and spinning. Men worked all around it, wearing overalls and helmets, every one of them filthy with oil. The central shaft kept roaring, making the whole deck vibrate. Other men were balanced on girders directly over the sea, tied securely to the structure with rope.

Schulman wanted to cover his ears. Instead he glanced down the moonpool. He saw the linked pipes running down and disappearing into the dark sea. That sight almost made him dizzy. It wasn't like being in the helicopter. When he saw the men above, tied to the structure with rope, hanging over that terrifying abyss, he had to admire them.

'What are they doing?' he asked.

'Removing the blow-back preventer,' Masters replied. 'It's a twenty-ton cube, but it's down four hundred feet and that makes it weigh four hundred tons. They're bringing it up, but they have to do it in forty-five-foot sections. They have to disconnect each pipe as it comes up and it's a hell of a job.'

The roaring stopped abruptly and the shaft whined to a standstill. On the girders, the men fixed huge clamps to the pipe and then attached thick chains to the clamps. The chains rattled and banged as the clamps made a dreadful screeching sound. The men were fixing large handles to the clamps as Masters walked from the hut.

Schulman followed him out and felt the blast of an icy wind. They were now on the main deck with its network of huge oil tanks and catwalks and thick, silver-painted flow-pipes. The derrick soared above the deck. Low clouds drifted over it. There were three platforms inside the derrick and the highest was the smallest. More men were working up there, looking minute and defenceless. The wind was howling between the girders of the derrick and making their overalls flap ceaselessly. Schulman glanced across the deck and saw more stacked pipes and oil tanks. Like everything else here, they were immense, soaring high above him. He followed Masters across the deck. A crane clanked and whined above them, swinging a stack of large wooden crates out over the sea with men hanging from the chains, giving the crane-driver hand signals.

Nearing the edge of the main deck, Masters waved Schulman forward. They both stopped when they were close to the rim, then Schulman looked down. He sucked in his breath automatically, then grabbed the railing beside him. The wind was beating at him, trying to push him off the edge, making him feel very vulnerable. The sea was very far below and he was looking down at a supply ship which, though immense, looked like a toy. Schulman felt a bit dizzy. It wasn't like being in the helicopter. The massive legs of the rig, running outwards and down, emphasized that dreadful plunge to the sea and made his head reel.

The crane was lowering the wooden crates, which were swinging to and fro. They swung under the decks and out again, each time dropping lower, with the roustabouts still balanced on them. Looking like ants on the chains, the men were now about a hundred feet down, still shouting and waving.

Schulman had to feel respect. He also felt a childish pride. His gaze fell upon the void between the men and the sea, then he saw the waves washing over the long, bobbing bulk of the loading ship, and that made him feel strange again. He turned away from those frightful depths. There was a sudden, savage roaring from the drilling hut and it gave him a shock. The enormous derrick towered over him.

Having just walked off the deck, Masters was framed by the sea and the sky as the wind howled about him. Then Schulman saw the platform thrusting out from the main deck. It was looming out over the sea and Masters stood on its far edge, at a bottle-shaped metal tank with a diving bell on the top. The diving bell was clamped on to the tank and the tank had round windows. It was a decompression chamber. Masters was at one of the windows. He gestured at someone inside, then put his thumb up. Schulman was loath to join him. He felt queasy at the very thought of it. He didn't want to go out there and be picked up by the wind and hurled down a couple of hundred feet to the sea. He was too young to die.

Another man walked past Schulman, off the deck and across the platform to Masters. He was wearing a white helmet and his overalls were smeared with oil. He grinned and shouted at Masters, glanced up and gesticulated. Schulman heard the appalling din of a crane, then saw a chain swinging into view. It stopped above Masters's head, above the decompression chamber. When the tool-pusher waved, two roustabouts rushed forward and clambered up the sides of the diving bell. There was a huge clamp on the chain, like a monstrous metal claw; it closed around the steel ring at the top of the diving bell and the roustabouts tightened screws all around it. Masters waved, left the platform and walked back up to Schulman. The men on top of the decompression chamber were checking the diving bell as the tool-pusher bellowed his instructions.

'It's the divers,' Masters explained. 'They're on saturation diving. We're going to lower them down there again, to check out the drilling point. They go down in the bell.'

'How deep?' Schulman asked.

'Four hundred feet.'

'Jesus,' Schulman hissed. 'How do they stand it?'

'It's a tough job,' Masters replied, meaning it, having himself gone down in a decompression chamber as part of his SBS training. 'That chamber's only ten foot long and there's six men inside it.'

'How long have they been in there?'

'Two weeks,' Masters told him. 'There's six

bunks in there. The men go down, the bell's hauled up when they're finished, it's attached to the top of the decompression chamber again, and then they go straight into the chamber.'

'You mean they *live* in that fucking thing for two weeks?'

'That's right. In the old days they would dive, undergo decompression, have a long break and then go down again. It was known as bounce diving. But now we can't afford that. We just don't have the time. Now we do saturation diving, which is what these men specialize in. The diver comes up and stays in the chamber until he needs to go down again. Since he doesn't step out into normal pressure at all, he doesn't have to be completely decompressed before he goes down again. He eats and sleeps in there. Food is sent in through the airlock. The pressure turns his voice girlish and the helium destroys his sense of taste. He lives and works there for a fortnight, then spends another week there decompressing. It's a hell of a life.'

Schulman looked back at the platform. The roustabouts were still on top of the decompression chamber, surrounding the diving bell. One of them put his thumb up. Masters waved them down, and they slid off the side of the metal chamber and hurried back to the main deck. The tool-pusher looked through a window, then grinned and jerked his own thumb up. He walked away from the platform and glanced up, then waved his right hand.

The crane whined into life, its winch clattering noisily. The chain went taut as it picked up the diving bell, which swung from side to side over the decompression chamber, dangling in the grey void of the sky with the sea far below. It dropped towards the water, bouncing gently against the platform. It had half disappeared when the sea started roaring.

'Jesus Christ!' Masters whispered.

The roaring started far below, then spread out and reverberated. The men all rushed automatically to the platform and grabbed hold of the railing. Suddenly, the whole deck tilted. The roar of the sea became much louder. They saw the waves leaping up and curving back down, to smash again and again over the loading ship. Then the roaring became an explosion, with water geysering up and outward. It was exploding out from under a pontoon leg and turning the sea wild.

Schulman couldn't believe it. The deck tilted to the left. The whole rig shook and he heard the exploding sea and saw a white wall of water. The water exploded upwards, a hundred feet high. It spread out like a great fan and crashed down on top of the loading ship, completely submerging it. Schulman glanced around at Masters and saw his wide eyes, his knuckles white on the railing, which slanted down alarmingly to the left. The whole deck was slipping. Then it jumped up and fell again. It was a quarter of a mile long and yet it was tilting and screeching insanely. Schulman saw the diving bell swinging out and in again. It crashed into the platform with a dreadful bang. Then Schulman saw the sea and the sky and found himself on his back.

'The diving bell! Get it in!'

Schulman felt himself sliding, heading feet first towards the edge. He couldn't breathe and his heart was racing wildly as he clawed at thin air. His hand found something solid, his fist closed around a chain. His head was spinning and the roaring was in his ears, though he could hear Masters shouting. Schulman swallowed hard and blinked, then gazed down at his own body. His feet were dangling over the edge of the deck and beyond the narrow platform tilted downwards. There the decompression chamber was nearly on its side, hanging out over the sea. He heard the shriek of tortured metal, the snapping of bolts, and saw the chamber's clamps splitting open. Men were shouting on all sides. He glanced down at the bell, which was swinging out from the tilting side. Masters was looking back up over his shoulder, bawling instructions at someone. The crane was winching up, but the bell swung out and in again and smashed against the deck.

'Jesus Christ! The crane's going!' Schulman yelled.

Hanging down the tilting side, the American rolled on to his belly. He pulled himself toward the crates piled high above him and heard the shriek of bending metal and the heavy rattling of chains. He pulled himself to his feet, and saw men running in all directions. Looking up, he saw the crane way above, slowly turning and tilting. It was making a fearsome sound, being torn from its support. The huge support was leaning far to the right with the crane sliding off it. Schulman couldn't believe it. The crane was fifty feet up. It was monstrous, a huge contraption and its jib, about to crash to the deck. Men bellowed and scattered. Metal shrieked as the crane broke loose. It seemed to hang in the air, the jib buckled and broke apart, then the whole mass of metal and chains exploded over the deck.

Someone screamed and Schulman blinked and saw the spinning bell. The chain snapped and the bell disappeared as it plunged to the sea. Then the noise became overpowering. The falling crane had smashed through the deck. A huge chain whipped through the air and the jib fell apart and enormous, jagged pieces of steel pipe started bouncing and clattering. These rolled off the edge of the deck and plunged towards the sea, smashing on their way down into wooden crates, which exploded and were torn from their moorings and crushed men as they plummeted into the water.

Schulman heard the dreadful screams. The deck shuddered beneath him. He looked up and heard the derrick groaning and saw its frame bending. 'Oh, my God!' he cried out.

'Schulman, move!' Masters bawled. Something grabbed Schulman, tearing him from the crates and pushing him forcefully forward. He knew it wasn't Masters, but he didn't stop to look back. Racing away from the derrick, he ran straight for the landing pad, hearing bawling and fearsome metallic screeching, and seeing chaos on all sides.

Something heavy crashed into the American, almost making his head explode. Recovering, he looked about him and saw enormous metal pipes breaking loose and rolling over the deck. They made a dreadful din, sweeping men and crates aside. Then Schulman glanced up and saw the towering derrick breaking apart and collapsing.

It was a terrible sight. The webbed beams were snapping free, bending and flying out and falling down and crashing into the drilling room. Schulman heard the demoniac noise, punctuated by the screams of the dying men. The derrick platforms fell apart and dropped down between the legs, then the legs themselves buckled and broke as the massive structure collapsed. Schulman looked up in awe. The spectacle froze him where he stood. There was an inferno of clanging steel and splintering wood and screaming men. Then the roof of the drilling room caved in and the noise grew even louder.

'On your feet! Get going!'

Galvanized by Masters's voice, Schulman started running, heading for the helicopter pad now sloping towards the sea. A sudden panic seized him. The helicopter had started moving. It was sliding towards the edge of the landing pad while slowly turning around. Schulman sobbed, but kept running. He didn't look back for Masters. He heard screams and passed other fleeing men, then saw a huge tank collapsing. It smashed through its supports and hit the deck with a fearsome sound. Though forty feet wide, the tank rolled rapidly across the deck to crush two men and crash into the modules and sweep the structures over the side.

Schulman didn't stop to help. He saw the helicopter slipping. A large wooden crate was racing towards him, shaking and screeching. It hit a tank and fell apart, the wood exploding in all directions. The yellow fork-lift inside it spun round and crashed into a catwalk, tearing it from its moorings. The catwalk buckled down the middle, bounced up in the air, rolled shrieking across the careering fork-lift and was finally dragged along with it. Schulman glimpsed waving arms and heard a terrible, dying scream. A decapitated body was mangled up in the spinning catwalk, limbs flailing in a gruesome dance as it went over the side.

But Schulman kept running up the sloping deck. Seeing the helicopter slipping towards the sea, he wanted to scream. Another roar, another crash. More explosions and colliding pipes. He heard bawling and saw shadowy, running figures as he reached the catwalk. The landing pad was tilting badly, its nearside swinging upwards, tearing the catwalk out of the deck and making its bolts snap. Without thinking, Schulman leapt forward to grab hold of the railing. Glancing down, he saw the sickening drop to the sea. Then Masters slapped his back and bawled something. The catwalk shuddered and its steel frame shrieked and bent as Schulman started his climb.

'It's broken loose!' Masters bellowed.

Schulman dived at the landing pad, hit the deck and rolled over. He heard the mangling of metal as the catwalk tore loose, then felt something fall across him and roll off. Blinking, he saw Masters sprawling beside him, then clambering back to his feet with great agility and rushing forward again.

The American sprang to his feet as the catwalk disappeared. The whole rig was now tilting towards the sea. Turning towards the landing pad, Schulman saw Masters at the helicopter, which was sliding dangerously close to the edge as he tugged its door open. Masters hauled himself up and Schulman raced up behind him. As Masters disappeared inside, the pilot hauled himself in and scrambled past him like a madman to get at the controls.

Schulman hardly knew what he was doing, but his training saw him through. The engines roared into life and the props picked up speed. Glanced out, he saw the deck veering down, the edge curving away from him. He worked the controls, felt a feverish, fearful clarity, then glanced down at the sea far below, the upturned loading ship and the drowning men.

Schulman tried to control the helicopter, but it swung towards the edge. The deck disappeared beneath him and he felt his stomach lurch. The helicopter dropped into space, fell a little, then rose again.

'Jesus Christ!' Masters groaned.

They climbed to eight hundred feet and hovered there to survey the wreckage. The huge rig was sinking down at the north-east corner, slipping into the sea, the massive deck a hideous mess of tangled steel and broken crates. A deluge of men and equipment was pouring over the sides. The corner of the rig sank, the sea boiling and swirling around it. The rest of the deck was pointing at the sky, swaying to and fro, before sinking slowly. Two pontoon legs surfaced, rising up three hundred feet in the air, and then slid under the water. The water churned and closed over them. A black hole materialized and turned into a whirlpool that imprisoned the men and machinery and sucked them all down. It was a ghastly, silent spectacle; a dark, eerie dream. The whirlpool swirled and sucked everything down and then folded in on itself.

Eventually the sea settled. It was calm and utterly desolate. Schulman looked down and saw nothing but those grey Arctic wastes.

'Head for the Forties Field,' Masters said.

4

The first interruption came in the middle of the Prime Minister's opening remarks. Keith Turner, sitting at the long table in the boardroom of Bravo 1, looked exasperated as he picked up the telephone. 'Excuse me, Prime Minister,' he said. 'I have to leave this line open.' He put the receiver to his ear and saw the Prime Minister watching him. He had never met the PM before, and found him intimidating.

There was some static on the line and Turner, the general supervisor of all the North Sea oil rigs, flushed with annoyance. He had told them specifically not to call him unless it was urgent. Now he heard the radio operator and it was clear that he was upset. 'I think you better get here right away. Eagle 3's in bad trouble,' the man said. Turner coughed into his fist and glanced apologetically around him. The PM had his chin in his hands and was staring straight at him.

'Trouble?' Turner asked. 'What kind of trouble?'

The boardroom was crowded. It overlooked the Forties Field. There were isolated oil rigs in the distance, and Turner couldn't stop staring at them. They suddenly filled his whole consciousness. The PM and his executives and the oil men and the secretaries – all disappeared from his vision and his thoughts as his heart started racing.

The operator's voice was high-pitched, almost hysterical. The man was babbling about a message from Eagle 3 and Turner sensed it was serious. He mumbled something to the operator, put the phone down, then glanced at the men all around him and shook imperceptibly.

'Excuse me, gentlemen,' he said, 'but I have to leave. We have an emergency.'

'Emergency?' someone repeated. It was Sir Reginald McMillan, the Chairman of British United Oil, and he was drumming his fingers. 'What *kind* of emergency?'

'I'm not sure, sir,' Turner said, standing up and tugging at his neat black beard. 'We've just had a call from Eagle 3 and I'll have to attend to it.'

He didn't wait to discuss it further. He wasn't too sure of what he'd heard. Smiling nervously, he rushed from the boardroom and headed straight for the radio shack. It took him quite a while to get there. Bravo 1 was immense; it was a platform with five drilling units and numerous decks. Turner hurried across the catwalks, feeling a warm, southerly wind. He saw the sea far below, all around him, and it gave him no comfort.

Could Eagle 3 really be sinking? The question rang in his head as he raced across a deck and wove his way between fork-lifts and modules. He felt the pounding of his heart and felt distinctly unreal. When he saw the antennae rising above the radio shack, he thought of the gibbering operator and felt even more concerned. Is Masters all right? he wondered, anxious about his SBS man. Then he opened the door of the radio shack and hurried inside.

The first thing that struck him when he entered was how pale the operator looked. The man was trying to contact Eagle 3. He was cursing as he looked up at Turner and took off his earphones.

'I can't get a response,' he said.

The radio shack was small and cluttered, uncomfortably hot and badly lit. The operator had his sleeves rolled up and was spattered with oil.

'They said they were *sinking*?' Turner queried, still not able to grasp it.

'That's right,' the operator replied. 'That guy on Eagle 3, he was practically screaming and he said they were sinking. There was a hell of a lot of static. His radio wasn't working properly. I asked for confirmation, but he just went demented. Repeated that they were sinking. Said they were going down fast. I tried to get some more details, but the line just went dead and I haven't been able to get them back since.'

'You didn't get any other calls?'

'No, chief, not one.'

Turner bit his lower lip and glanced anxiously about him. This was something he didn't want to accept; it just didn't seem possible. How could it sink so suddenly? What the hell had gone wrong? A rig didn't just sink in a matter of minutes . . . Turner tugged at his black beard, his broad bulk trembling slightly, then he blinked and looked down at the operator, trying to order his thoughts.

'Any other calls from Eagle 3 this morning? Any messages at all?'

'No. We've been keeping the lines clear. All the rigs had instructions not to call except in an emergency.'

'No message from Masters?'

'Not a thing, chief. The first call I got was from Eagle 3 – and he said they were sinking.'

'I don't believe it,' Turner said. 'An accident, yes, I can accept that; but I can't see it sinking.'

'It sounded like it,' the operator said. 'That fucking guy was hysterical. And his radio was really in a mess, even before it went off. Since then, nothing, and that can't be a good sign.'

'Bloody hell,' Turner said. He reached for a telephone, punched out a number, and glanced distractedly out of the open door at the sea. 'Hello,

Jackson? Turner here. I want a helicopter over the Frigg Field to survey Eagle 3 . . . No, not from here. That would take too long. What's the closest rig in the Beryl Field?' He drummed his fingers on the desk, then nodded and put the phone down. 'OK,' he said to the operator. 'Ring Charlie 2. Tell them to get their chopper to Eagle 3 and check out what's happening.'

The operator nodded and put on his earphones. Turner walked out of the radio shack and looked up at the sky, wondering what the hell was happening out there. The afternoon light was hazy. The southerly wind was turning cold. He suddenly remembered the conference in the boardroom and his stomach churned.

Could the rig have gone down? The possibility was enough to make him shiver with a fearful fatigue. He wouldn't tell anyone yet. He would keep it quiet until he knew. The very thought of having to announce such a catastrophe was beyond his imagining.

The operator came to the doorway to stare at him with wide, disbelieving eyes.

'I can't get them,' he said.

'What?'

'I can't get them. I can't get in touch with Charlie 2.'

'What the hell do you mean?'

'I can't get them to reply. Their line's open,

but there's no answer. They're just not replying.'

Turner could hardly believe his ears. He glanced out at the murky sea. When he turned back, he saw that the operator was scared and confused.

'You mean there's no one at their radio? The operator isn't there? Are you trying to say there's no one on duty?'

The operator threw up his hands. 'I just can't get a reply. I'm saying that the line's definitely open, but they just won't reply.'

'This is crazy!' Turner exploded.

'Yeah, it's crazy. I know.'

'For Christ's sake, keep on trying,' Turner said. 'What the hell's going on?'

The operator disappeared and Turner paced up and down beneath the modules that had been piled upon modules as this platform had grown bigger. He was dwarfed by its immensity. The five derricks towered above him. The grey sky loured beyond them, the sea was all around them and the silence of the platform was eerie. None of the drills was in operation; they hadn't been working for weeks. Nevertheless, the enormous platform was busy, working as a refinery. Men were hurrying across the catwalks. Cranes and fork-lifts were in action. New buildings were still being erected. Turner looked all around him, surveying his vast domain. He pondered the riddle of Eagle 3 and Charlie 2 and it didn't make sense.

He went back to the radio shack. 'What the fuck's going on?' he snapped, more to himself than to the operator, who lifted his left hand and waved him into silence, then said: 'OK. Roger and out.' The operator switched to Receive, placed his earphones on the table, swivelled around in his chair and stared straight at Turner.

'Charlie 2?' Turner asked.

'No. That was Masters.'

'Eagle 3?'

'No. In a chopper. He says he's coming in now.'

Feeling confused and fearful, Turner fiddled with his beard and glanced through the open door. There was no sign of the helicopter. Sighing, he turned back to the operator and noticed again how pale he looked.

'Did he say anything other than that?' he asked.

'Yes,' the operator replied. 'He asked if you were here.'

'Did he say anything about Eagle 3?'

'He said to tell you to be here.'

That wasn't like Masters. It sounded like a command. Turner cursed and paced back and forth, trying to order his thoughts.

'What about Charlie 2?' he asked.

'There's still no reply.'

'What's going on?' Turner asked, his tone more resigned now. 'I don't get the connection.'

He left the radio shack, climbed down a steel ladder, then crossed the deck between towering blocks of modules, and skirted around the soaring steel derricks. The wind was growing colder and the sea rose and fell. He passed some men on an enormous pile of pipes, then walked beneath a raised crane. Turner felt his heart pounding. He didn't like to feel this nervous. He reached the end of the deck, climbed up another ladder, then mounted the steel catwalk to the landing pad.

The Bravo 1 helicopter was parked there, beside an empty space. Turner went to the phone in a booth near the landing pads. He rang a tool-pusher, Dwight Bascombe, and told him to send up two roustabouts. Having done so, he put the phone back on its cradle and walked to the empty landing pad. He looked up at the sky and saw the Eagle 3 helicopter descending.

Turner cursed and paced the deck, keeping his eye on the helicopter. The two roustabouts came up the catwalk, wearing bright yellow overalls. They nodded at Turner, then glanced up at the sky. The Wessex Mk 3 was dropping towards them, sounding muffled and distant. The roustabouts went to work, unlocking the holding clamps. When they were finished, they stepped back beside Turner and, like him, looked up at the approaching helicopter.

It was roaring right above them now, its props whipping the wind about them. They held on to the railings of the catwalk and watched it come down. It landed with some precision, bouncing only a little. Its engines stopped and the props turned more slowly and then the side door opened.

Masters emerged first. Schulman followed him too quickly. The broken features of the tool-pusher's face were like granite and his brown hair was windswept. He hurried towards Turner with the pilot close behind him, letting the other passengers disembark by themselves, most looking dazed. Turner noticed that Schulman was drained of colour and looked scared. The roustabouts went to work, blocking and clamping the chopper's wheels. Masters walked up to Turner and stared at him with bright, anguished eyes.

'Eagle 3 has gone down,' he said.

Turner didn't know what to say. It seemed incomprehensible. He swallowed and then glanced at Schulman, who seemed physically ill. There was shock and disbelief on the American's face and he was visibly shaking. Then Turner stared hard at Masters, who nodded and turned to Schulman. He told him to go down to the bar and get himself a stiff drink. The pilot did what he was told, turning away without a word. They watched him go along the sloping catwalk and enter one of the modules. Then Masters went to the phone and rang through to the doctor. He told him to go down to the bar and take a look at Schulman. When he had done so, he hung up the phone and turned back to Turner.

'What happened?' Turner asked.

'It went down,' Masters replied. He took Turner by the elbow and led him away from the listening roustabouts. They stopped beneath the catwalk, above the murmuring of the sea. Masters ran his fingers through his short brown hair and glanced sharply about him. 'We were bombed,' he said quietly.

Turner felt a little dazed. He also felt a creeping chill. He was trying hard not to think of the Prime Minister and of what he might have to tell him.

'Jesus,' Turner said.

'Yeah,' replied Masters. 'Some bastard planted a bomb in the north-east pontoon leg.'

'A bomb?'

'You've got it – a bomb. It blew a hole in the leg, the platform tilted, and the whole rig went crazy.'

'It's totally gone?' Turner asked.

'Yep. The whole rig fell apart and then it sank and took everything with it.'

'No survivors?'

'Apart from the few in the helicopter, no. No other survivors.'

'My God,' Turner said. He looked at the other man's eyes, which were glinting with shock and anger. They kept flitting back and forth around the deck, as if searching for clues. 'Who the hell . . . ?'

'I don't know,' Masters said. 'I've considered various possibilities, but most don't make sense.'

'It had to be someone on the rig.'

'You're pretty smart,' Masters said.

'A fanatic. Someone who didn't care if he went down with the rig. Some dumb bastard who wants to be a martyr.'

'Maybe,' Masters said. 'But he didn't have to go down with it. He might have used a long-delay timer. He didn't have to be there himself.'

'*Why?*' Turner asked.

'The Prime Minister,' Masters suggested. 'The time and dates can't have been accidental. It's just too close for comfort.'

'But why Eagle 3? It's a hundred and fifty miles north.'

'I know. It doesn't add up. There must be something else coming.'

Turner glanced around him, drawn by the sea's murmuring. He tried to focus on the roustabouts and roughnecks swarming over the platform.

'They're still in conference?' Masters asked.

'Jesus Christ, don't remind me.'

'Do they know?'

'No, they don't. They know there's an emergency, but they don't know what it is and I doubt whether they suspect the extent of it.'

'What about the radio operator?'

'Well, he knows it went down. He knows that, but he doesn't know what happened. Your man didn't get that far.'

'OK,' Masters said. 'We better make him stay quiet. We can say there's been a very bad accident. We needn't say what it was.'

'A bomb,' Turner said distractedly. 'Jesus Christ. Do you think it's us next?'

'I doubt it,' Masters said. 'I mean, I really can't believe it. This whole platform was checked from top to bottom – by your men *and* the SBS. Our divers were down there today. We've got cameras on the seabed. We've X-rayed every crate and every pipe, and the boardroom's well guarded. No, I don't think it will be here. I don't believe so. But I still can't work it out.'

'Why Eagle 3?' Turner asked for the second time. 'They must have known it was closing down. Why the hell would they plant a bomb on Eagle 3? They must be out of their minds.'

'I can't figure it out,' Masters said, staring at the ground.

'Charlie 2,' Turner recalled. 'When we heard what had happened, we tried to get in touch, but they simply wouldn't answer our calls.'

Masters jerked his head up and stared hard at Turner. 'You received no reply from Charlie 2? You think *they* might have sunk as well?'

'No,' Turner replied. 'The line was clearly open. Their radio was definitely turned on.' He shrugged. 'They just wouldn't respond.'

'Oh, my God,' Masters said.

He hurried away. Turner blinked and rushed after him. They walked across the main deck, past the stacked pipes and crates, beneath the cranes, around the derricks and modules, to a vertical ladder, which Masters climbed with practised ease. Turner followed and stood beside him on the platform, where the wind moaned about them. Masters massaged his forehead, blinked, rubbed his eyes, looked briefly at the leaden sky and the sea, then studied the radio shack.

'Let's keep it quiet for now,' he said. 'The last thing we want is panic. Let's just say there was a very bad accident and we're working it out.'

'An explosion,' Turner suggested. 'We'll say the well-head exploded. We'll say a pile of oil drums went up with it and caused complete chaos.'

'Charlie 2,' Masters said. 'There must be a connection. They wouldn't leave the radio open. They wouldn't just walk away.'

'Jesus Christ,' Turner whispered.

'It's on the pipeline,' Masters said. 'The main pipe runs from Frigg down to Beryl and then on to the Forties.'

'You mean terrorists?'

'Yes.'

'Jesus Christ, that's impossible!'

'There's no security on Beryl or Frigg. The security's here.'

'The *Prime Minister's* here!'

'That's correct: he's right here.'

'Then why Beryl? Why Frigg? I don't get it. It doesn't add up.'

'It just might,' Masters said, glancing intently around him. 'There's a floating refinery on Beryl and the pipe runs to here.'

'Then why Frigg?' Turner asked.

'The Frigg supply runs through Beryl. The oil extracted from Frigg goes to Beryl and then on to here.'

'But Frigg's drying up.'

'That's right, it's drying up.'

'Then why would they want to cut off Eagle 3 if the field's drying up?'

'I don't know,' Masters said.

He started walking again, heading for the radio shack. When he entered, Turner followed him in and the operator looked up, surprised. He was very pale. Staring at Masters, he opened his mouth to speak, then nervously cleared his throat.

'I've got Charlie 2,' he said. 'They want to speak to you, Masters. I asked for the message and they wouldn't give it. Instead, they told me to find you.'

'There's been an accident,' Masters told him.

'They sounded weird, chief. It wasn't the usual guy – it was McGee, and he sounded really strange.'

'What did he say?' Masters asked.

'Nothing,' the operator replied, glancing from Masters to Turner, clearly confused. 'He just said: "Go and get Masters." What's happening out there?'

'There's been an accident,' Turner lied. 'An explosion on Frigg. We're still trying to find out what caused it, so we want it kept quiet.'

The operator looked relieved. Shaking his head, he offered a tentative grin, then slowly stood up.

'Oh,' he said. 'I see. I mean, I thought it was just me. I thought maybe I'd done something wrong and I just couldn't work it out.'

'It's classified,' Masters told him. 'Accidents like this always are. We have to check it out thoroughly and put in a report. It has to be strictly confidential.'

'I understand, chief.'

'Make sure you do,' Masters warned him. 'If I hear the slightest word from the crew, you'll be out of a job.'

The operator licked his lips and nodded.

'Go outside,' Turner told him. 'Close the door when you leave. Stay out there and don't let anyone in. Is that understood?'

'Yes, chief,' the operator said, then hurried out of the radio shack. When the door was closed, Masters sat at the table and put on the earphones.

'Bravo 1 to Charlie 2,' Masters said. 'Are you receiving me?'

Turner heard the crackling radio. He couldn't hear what was being said. He heard Masters, but he couldn't hear Charlie 2 – only the static.

'Bravo 1,' Masters said. 'Yes, it's Masters. Let me speak to McGee.'

Turner paced up and down, feeling dazed and ill. He was nervous and he looked down at Masters with a singular sympathy. Masters listened for a long time. His hands were steady on the table. He had large hands and long, calloused fingers which didn't move once. Turner found the shack stifling. He paced up and down the short, narrow room and tried to empty his mind. Then he heard Masters curse and saw him put the earphones down. The tool-pusher swivelled around in his chair and looked at Turner with piercing eyes.

'It's McGee,' Masters said. 'He's got a terrorist group on board. He says they've also got a plutonium bomb on board – and they're willing to use it.'

'Jesus Christ!' Turner groaned. 'Oh, my God! What the hell do they want?'

'They want the Prime Minister.'

5

Masters and Turner were both sitting by the radio when Robert Barker entered the shack. He saw the sweat on Turner's forehead and the tension on the tool-pusher's face. He had not seen Masters so tense before, so he knew it was bad.

'OK,' Barker said, 'what's the emergency?'

'It's bad,' Masters said.

'I gathered that, Tone. I'm supposed to be protecting the Prime Minister, so what the hell is it?'

'We were bombed,' Masters said. 'Eagle 3 has been sunk. Now a bunch of terrorists has taken over Charlie 2 and they've got a plutonium bomb.'

Barker was silent for a moment, trying to take in this ghastly tale. He didn't have to ask if it was true; he could tell by looking at the two men's faces.

'Bombed?' he asked nevertheless, needing confirmation. 'How the hell did they do it?'

'They bombed one of the legs of a pontoon and the whole rig went down.'

'Oh, my God.'

'It's the IRA,' Masters explained. 'There's a

foreman on Charlie 2 called McGee and the cunt's a terrorist.'

Suddenly, Barker felt claustrophobic. The radio shack wasn't well lit and it felt like a Turkish bath. He glanced from Masters to Turner and saw the sweat on the latter's forehead. The supervisor was drumming his fingertips on the table, staring at the radio.

'Why Eagle 3?' Barker asked.

'I don't know yet,' Masters said. 'I didn't get a chance to ask that question. They want the Prime Minister.'

'The Prime Minister,' Barker repeated flatly.

'That's right: the PM. They say they'll blow up Charlie 2 – and if they have to, they'll do it – if we don't let them speak to the PM. They've got a plutonium bomb on board. McGee said they would use it. I don't know how they managed it, but they've taken over the whole of Charlie 2.'

'You mean they've hijacked the rig?'

'Looks like it.'

'How many?'

'I don't know.'

'There's eighty men on that rig.'

'I know. I don't know how they did it, but they've certainly taken it.'

Barker whistled, patted his blond hair and shook his head from side to side.

'God,' he said, 'this is bad. It's fucking disastrous.

If they say they're willing to go down with Charlie 2, then they probably mean it. Fucking IRA lunatics!'

'It's McGee,' Masters said. 'He seems to be the leader. He said: "This is an official announcement from the IRA. We've hijacked your rig." He didn't bother explaining any more. He just said he wanted to speak to the Prime Minister, but he'd speak to you first.'

'Bastard,' Barker said.

'He's not kidding,' Masters told him. 'He could be bluffing, but he certainly isn't kidding – and he *did* blow up Eagle 3. They probably used a long-delay timer with the primer on Charlie 2.'

'Some of the crew,' Barker suggested. 'The rig workers aren't checked out. I've been wanting to run checks on them for years, but the bigwigs wouldn't let me.'

'They will in future,' Turner said.

'Fucking great,' Barker responded. 'In the meantime it costs us two rigs and now they want the PM.'

'That's right,' Masters said.

'It's impossible,' Turner said. 'We can't even let him know this has happened. We can't let the word out.'

'It'll get out,' Barker insisted.

'Not immediately,' Turner replied. 'The PM's in conference and we'll let him stay there until we manage to sort this mess out. We can't tell him till then.'

Barker looked at the floor. 'Let me get this straight. The terrorists have bombed Eagle 3. They've taken over Charlie 2. We don't know how, but they've managed to gain control and now they've got a plutonium bomb. Where the hell did they get the bomb? How on earth did they take the rig? There's eighty men in that crew and you don't buy plutonium bombs for peanuts. Have they got any proof?'

'I don't know,' Masters said. 'McGee wouldn't discuss it with me. He just said he wasn't kidding, that he wanted the PM, and that he was willing to speak to you first.'

'The PM's impossible.'

'That's what he wants, Barker.'

'It's not feasible,' Barker said. 'He must be bluffing. He's just trying it on.'

'Maybe,' Turner said.

'Maybe not,' Masters said. 'But the only way we're going to find out is to get on that radio.'

Barker glanced up and smiled, chuckled sardonically, shook his head, then paced up and down the cramped hut, pursing his lips. He stopped after a short while.

'OK, I'll talk. Let's hear what they have to say. We'll hold them off as long as we can and keep the PM out of it.' He studied the radio. 'Has that got an open line?' Turner nodded and reached out and flicked a switch. 'Now we'll all hear,' he said. Barker nodded and said: 'That's what I want.'

Turner leant forward and spoke into the microphone, keeping his voice low and level. 'Bravo 1 to Charlie 2. Bravo 1 to Charlie 2. Are you receiving me?' There was the crackling of static, swelling up and fading out. 'Charlie 2 to Bravo 1, we're receiving. We don't want you, Turner. We want Barker.' Turner couldn't help grinning at Barker as he got out of the chair. Barker distractedly smoothed his hair as he sat down at the microphone.

'OK,' he said, 'it's Barker. Put McGee on.'

There was silence for a moment, apart from the crackling static. Barker placed his elbow on the table and rested his chin in his cupped hands. Turner moved sideways to stand close by Masters. Their eyes met, then they both stared at the radio, feeling tense and defeated.

'Barker?' a voice on the radio asked.

'Yes, this is Barker.'

'This is McGee. I'm speaking on behalf of the Irish Republican Army. I'm officially notifying you that we've requisitioned Charlie 2 on behalf of the IRA for the . . .'

'Cut the shit,' Barker interjected. 'What do you want?'

'Our demands will only be given to the Prime Minister. We won't settle for less.'

'You can't speak to the Prime Minister. It's impossible and you know it. There's no way I'm going to bring him into this and that's all there is to it.'

'You'll give us what we want,' McGee said, 'or suffer the consequences.'

'Which are?'

'We've captured Charlie 2. We've got a plutonium bomb on board. We won't hesitate to set the bomb off if we don't get satisfaction. Don't attempt to attack the rig. If we see any ships or helicopters, we'll set the bomb off.'

'Do that and you'll blow yourselves up as well.'

'We don't care, Barker. We're willing to go down with the rig. And you all know enough about the IRA to know we mean what we say.'

'I don't believe you,' Barker said. 'You couldn't find a plutonium bomb. If you did, you couldn't transport it to the rig without being detected. I think you're bluffing.'

'Eagle 3 was no bluff. It was a demonstration and warning. It was a much smaller bomb on Eagle 3, but this one is the real thing. We didn't find it – we made it. They're surprisingly easy to make. The finished product is only thirty-six inches long and it doesn't weigh much. It was easy getting it on the rig. In fact, it's been on board for months. It only weighs half a ton and it was put in a packing crate and shipped out from Aberdeen with the regular equipment. I'm the foreman on this rig. Your tool-pushers are all my mates. We shipped it in with the regular supplies and now it's all set to blow.'

'I don't believe you,' Barker said.

'You don't have to,' McGee replied. 'We've left the proof for you to find. Get your onshore security team to check out the Aberdeen heliport. Tell them to check the toilets, third one from the door, and look behind the cistern. I left a brown envelope there. It contains full details of the design and construction of the bomb. Ask them to check it out. They'll soon confirm that it's authentic. When they ring you back with that confirmation we'll be able to deal.'

Barker studied the microphone. He covered his face with his right hand. After rubbing his eyes, he glanced at Masters and shook his head in despair.

'OK,' he said finally. 'We'll check it out.'

'You have one hour,' McGee told him. 'I won't give you any longer. If I don't hear back in that time I'm gonna blow up this rig. You know what that means, Barker. The blast will destroy the whole of Beryl, wiping it out completely. It'll also cause a lot of damage to the Forties Field. And the supply pipes will go with it. You'll lose two-thirds of the North Sea oil. There'll be enough contamination to ensure you can't work this sea for years. Think about that while you're waiting.'

Masters glanced at Turner. The supervisor was

visibly shaken, leaning against the door of the radio shack, wiping sweat from his brow. Masters then studied his friend Robert Barker. The chief security man of British United Oil was tapping the table gently with his fingertips as he stared at the radio.

'How many men have you got?' Barker asked.

'Sixty,' McGee replied. 'They were all regular crew members. We've been working on this plan for eighteen months, so we'd plenty of time. Your chief tool-pusher's my man. He's been with us from the start. He's the man who hires and fires and he's gradually been replacing your men with ours, as well as a lot of Scottish nationalists who're helping us out for their own ends.'

'I don't think you could have managed that,' Barker said, though he didn't sound hopeful.

'Rig workers aren't asked questions. As well you know, Barker, any man who's willing to work on a rig will be hired without question. You never approved of it. Too bad your superiors didn't listen. It's taken us eighteen months and we had to use the Scots, but now we've got sixty of our own men on board and we've executed most of the remaining crew.'

'You bastard,' Barker said.

'We spared two,' McGee said. 'I thought you might want a few witnesses, so there's two still alive. One's John Griffith, your geologist. He's standing right beside me now. You want proof, so I'm gonna put him on and you can ask what you like.'

Masters felt himself burning with a murderous rage. He smacked his fist against his hand and turned away to stare out through the window. The afternoon light was dull. The North Sea was calm. It stretched out to the horizon, towards the Beryl Field, then was lost in a misty haze. Masters turned back again when he heard the voice of Griffith coming over the radio.

'Barker?'

'Yes, Griffith.'

'It's true, Barker. All true. They've got about sixty men on this rig and they've taken it over.' Griffith's voice was shaky and high-pitched. 'They killed the remaining crew. Took them up on deck and shot them. They just shot them and threw them over the side and they made us two watch it.' Griffith stopped and seemed to sob. They heard him trying to control himself. Masters clenched his fists and stared at the radio, wanting to smash it. 'They're serious,' Griffith continued. 'They mean every word they say. They spared me and Sutton, but they killed all the others and dumped them into the sea. Oh, dear God, I just don't . . .'

Barker lowered his head. They all listened to Griffith sobbing. Masters clenched his fists and Turner turned away, looking like death warmed up.

'Bastards!' he whispered. Griffith's sobbing faded out as McGee started talking again.

'Is that enough for you, Barker? Are you satisfied? Or do you want to hear more?'

'No, that's enough. I don't want to hear any more.'

'You have one hour,' McGee repeated, then he cut the connection.

Barker turned off his receiver, pushed back his chair, and stood up, deep in thought.

'Well?' Masters asked. 'Do I call in the SBS and try to take that rig back?'

'Not yet,' Barker said. 'Not if they've got a plutonium bomb on board. I can't believe they've made a working nuclear bomb, but we'll have to find out first. I'll ring Andy Blackburn. He's the best man I have. I'll tell him not to use the local police, but to use our own security men instead. We have to keep this thing private. We don't want the regular Army or police involved. If word got out that a bunch of terrorists had managed to do all this, the repercussions internationally would be disastrous. Jesus, it's so *stupid*! We've no security on these damn rigs. We've actually *hired* sixty terrorists over the past eighteen months and I don't think we could ever live that down. We *can't* let the news out. We've got to solve it on our own. We've got to check if that bloody bomb works and then take it from there. I'll ring Andy right now.'

Barker picked up the telephone and rang the heliport. He spoke to Andy Blackburn, told him what to look for, then told him not to ask any questions and to keep his mouth shut. Masters stood there and listened. Barker gave nothing away. Masters gazed out the window and tried hard to control his boiling rage. His hands opened and closed, clutched the air and released it. He looked out at the sea and thought of Griffith and Sutton on that rig. The terrorists had sunk Eagle 3. Most of the crew had gone down with it. The terrorists had murdered twenty men on Charlie 2 and thrown them over the side. Masters felt like exploding, like smashing the radio shack. He heard Barker speaking into the phone, sounding calm and collected. Then Barker rang off. He turned around to face Turner. The bearded supervisor was chewing a matchstick and sweating profusely.

'OK,' Barker said, 'he's going to check. In the meantime, we wait.'

6

Convinced that the situation should be kept secret as long as possible, Turner decided to return to the boardroom. Walking across the main deck, seeing the rig workers all around him, he felt himself succumbing to panic. The terrorists had a plutonium bomb. They could obliterate the Beryl Field. The bomb could also devastate the Forties Field and set them back a good ten years. The results would be catastrophic. The whole of Britain could collapse. When he pictured the faces in the boardroom, Turner felt like a drowning man.

He reached the end of the deck, started climbing the steel steps, and saw dull clouds passing slowly over the sea as if nothing had changed.

Turner didn't want to do it. The thought of the boardroom made him ill. He would have to go in there and lie, and the thought made his heart pound. He wished that Masters was there with him. The SBS trooper had the strength he needed. But what would happen when Blackburn called? What could they do if the bomb worked? Turner desperately tried to find a way out as he climbed the ladder.

He reached the upper deck, opened the door of the nearest module, stepped inside and closed the door behind him, then took a deep breath and walked on.

Not believing he could face the meeting, he was trembling when he reached the boardroom. The guard opened the door and Turner felt himself smiling, putting on a casual mask as he walked in. Then the panic disappeared. It simply fell away from him. He walked over to the table, sat down in his chair and gazed calmly around him.

'Sorry, gentlemen,' he heard himself saying. 'A spot of bother on the Frigg Field.'

The Prime Minister, who had been talking, went quiet and glanced up. Turner noticed that his eyes were very blue, with a cold, hard intelligence.

'Oh?' the PM said. 'I'm sorry to hear that. Anything serious?'

'We're not sure yet,' Turner replied. 'We think a well-head exploded. We don't know how much damage it caused, but we're having it checked out.'

Tapping a pencil on the table, Sir Reginald McMillan stared at him. He was slim, grey-haired and distinguished, with a pale, remote face. 'An explosion?' he asked.

'Yes, sir,' Turner said.

'Dearie me. What rig was this?'

'Eagle 3,' Turner said.

Sir Reginald glanced at the PM. Clearly the news hadn't pleased him. Sir Reginald turned his pencil over and started doodling, then looked over at Turner. 'What happened?' he asked.

'We don't know, sir. They're still trying to sort it out. Apparently some oil drums exploded, which has made it all the worse. We're waiting for further news and they're ringing us back as soon as possible. I've left Masters in charge, but I'll probably have to go up there again. I hope you'll excuse me.'

'Of course,' Sir Reginald said. 'Who's this Masters?'

Turner hesitated. Apart from Robert Barker, he was the only man in the company who knew that Tony Masters was one of the many SBS men working under cover on the oil rigs. He wasn't sure that the PM knew about the SBS involvement; if he didn't, he might be outraged to learn about it by accident. Discretion being the better part of valour, Turner decided to keep his mouth shut on this particular issue.

'A top tool-pusher,' he said. 'He's one of our best men. He's handled situations like this before and knows what he's doing.'

Sir Reginald sighed, trying to hide his annoyance. Such accidents could happen, but it was dreadful to have one at a time like this. He glanced at the PM and saw those blue eyes staring at him with a mixture of accusation and pleasure. Of course, the PM would try to use the accident as a stick to beat the oil companies with. Any suggestion of negligence would strengthen his government's bargaining position.

'An explosion?' the PM asked like a perfect innocent. 'Is this sort of thing common?'

'No, Prime Minister,' Turner said. 'It does happen, but very seldom. The North Sea's very deep and the pressure is tremendous and that obviously leads to the unexpected. It's happened before and it'll happen again, but it's by no means common.'

'I see,' the PM said.

'It's in the Frigg Field,' Sir Reginald explained. 'Luckily the explosion was on Eagle 3, which is closing down anyway.'

'Closing down?' the PM asked.

'Yes, Prime Minister, closing down. Eagle 3 was drying up and was due to be towed away to another field. The blow-up therefore won't be as bad as it might have been, since to all intents and purposes the rig was closed. Had she been operating it might well have been worse.'

'That *was* lucky,' the PM said brightly.

'Yes, Prime Minister, very lucky. That no oil was coming out of Eagle 3 was very lucky indeed.'

Sir Reginald's smile was not returned by the PM. Instead, the PM glanced in turn at each of the other men, who were all sleek and well-fed. These were the oil magnates, representing the conglomerates. They headed individual companies that were part of larger companies and the source of their power was elusive. They were an international crew, living in boardrooms and hotels, reporting behind closed doors to unknown superiors, not intimidated by politicians or the rule of law. The PM didn't like them because they had rendered his government impotent. He could never forget that fact.

'Anyone hurt?' he asked.

'We don't know yet,' Turner replied. 'I would anticipate casualties, but we won't know until they ring back.'

'They seem slow,' the Under-Secretary said.

'They're fighting the fire,' Turner told him.

'I trust we'll receive a full report.'

'Of course, sir. That's our policy.'

The Under-Secretary smiled thinly. He sensed that Turner was being too calm. He knew that accidents on the rigs were handled by the oil companies and that the reports were written up by their own men. The Under-Secretary did not approve. He knew the reports could not be trusted. He felt that the Department of Energy should be called in at such times to conduct an independent investigation. He had been fighting for this for years, but it was a fight he hadn't won. The oil companies had resisted all attempts to uncover their skeletons.

'What's happening now?' he asked.

'We're simply waiting,' Turner replied. 'I've left Masters in the radio shack with instructions to call me.'

'Excellent,' Paul Dalton said, smiling encouragingly at Turner. He was a rough-looking, suntanned American with a shock of red hair. 'I've met Masters and think he's a good man – completely trustworthy. The guy has an air of authority.'

Knowing that this 'air of authority' had been instilled by the SBS, Turner was relieved to receive Dalton's support, which would, he hoped, deflect any further questions about Masters. Dalton was one of the American top dogs, so his word carried weight here. He had worked his way up the hard way, first as a roustabout, as a roughneck and tool-pusher, then as head of security for American oil companies in Saudi Arabia and New Mexico. Now he was one of the most powerful men in the business, a top-flight executive who worked for most of the conglomerates, the kind who made lesser men uneasy, particularly because they didn't know his specific function nor precisely for whom he was working. They only knew that he was free to roam the world at will, dropping in on any oilfield, company office or headquarters, and that he did so with alarming frequency. Where Dalton went, heads invariably rolled, which made him all the more frightening. His presence at this top-level conference had put them all, even the PM, on their toes.

'Masters is good,' Dalton insisted. 'He's really good. I don't doubt we can trust him.'

'I agree,' Turner said. 'He's been through this kind of thing before and knows how to deal with it. He also knows what to do when the rig calls: he'll send someone to fetch me.'

'Will they need help?' Sir Reginald asked, meaning the men on the rig he thought was only damaged.

'We won't know until they call back,' Turner said. 'In the meantime, we'll sit tight.'

'Fine by me,' Dalton said.

'Most unfortunate,' Sir Reginald murmured.

'So,' the PM said firmly, trying to avoid Dalton's steely gaze, 'let's get back to business.'

The conference continued with voices arguing back and forth as the smoke from cigars and cigarettes drifted over their heads. Turner heard himself talking, but hardly knew what he was saying, being too busy looking through the portholes at the rigs in the distance. Was the Forties Field safe? Could Barker be sure of his security? Could they be certain there wasn't a terrorist right here in their midst? Should he not say to hell with it all and call in Masters's fellow SBS men? Turner heard the PM's voice, then Sir Reginald and then himself. His own voice seemed to come from far away, though it sounded surprisingly calm and reassuring. Turner gazed through the portholes. Rigs were smoking on the horizon. They were miles apart and looked very small, isolated, defenceless . . . Turner shivered. He tried to focus on the conference. He thought bitterly of the terrorists on Charlie 2 and he wished that the phone would ring.

When it rang, he felt paralysed.

7

Robert Barker knew the news wasn't good when he saw Turner's face. Turner was back in the radio shack, standing opposite Masters. Neither of them looked happy. When Barker entered, Turner looked out the window and Masters offered a tight smile.

'Well?' Barker asked.

'Blackburn thinks the bomb would work,' Masters told him. 'He found the photos and technical data behind the cistern in the toilet of the heliport, as McGee had said he would. He took them to the Aberdeen munitions lab of British United Oil. They phoned him five minutes ago and said they thought it would work.'

'Are they certain?' Barker asked.

'They can't be, but they're pretty sure. It's about the size of a tea chest, it weighs approximately a quarter of a ton, it's got everything it needs, all the pieces are in the right place, and with a minimum of luck it would work.'

'Jesus!' Turner gasped. He was looking out at the darkening Forties Field.

'OK,' Barker said. 'It's a workable design for a plutonium bomb, but that doesn't mean the bastards could actually make it. They're terrorists, not scientists. They're a bunch of killers. To design a bomb like this is one thing; to actually make it is another. Where did they get the materials? How did they put it all together? And how the hell would they manage to test it? The drawings by themselves don't mean they've got one.'

'You'd be surprised,' Masters said, thinking of the many extraordinary explosive devices created secretly in RM Commando demolition establishments. 'According to Blackburn, they're relatively easy to make, not that expensive, and becoming more common every day. He says that schoolkids have made them. He says that all the materials can be bought in the open market and that a large bomb, a workable one, is not out of the question. The plans McGee left were perfect. The lab thought the bomb could work. True, we don't know if he's actually made it, but we'd be safest to assume that he has.'

Barker smacked his forehead, then shook his head in disbelief. He walked to the door of the hut and then came back again.

'We have to know for sure,' he said. 'We have to know if they have a bomb on that rig or if they're trying to bullshit us.'

'Blackburn's on to it,' Masters said. 'He's trying

to find out right now. He's going to check out McGee's movements over the past few months and try to come up with more concrete information. In the meantime, we'll have to accept that they might have that bomb.'

'Which means that even your SBS commandos can't make an assault on that rig.'

'Unfortunately not,' Masters said.

'Let's talk to McGee,' Barker suggested. 'Try to sound him out. To stretch it out a bit longer and give Blackburn more time.' He looked at Turner, who nodded and stepped aside. Barker sat at the radio and switched it on, engaging the open line. An unfamiliar voice asked him who he was and he said tersely: 'Barker. Now get me McGee.' After a long silence they heard the crackling of static, a snatch of laughter in the background, then someone coughing.

'Is that Barker?' McGee asked.

'Yes, McGee, this is Barker. You told me to call you back in an hour, so I'm calling you back.'

'I'm glad you listened,' McGee said. 'It shows common sense. I didn't like the thought of what would happen if you didn't show that.'

'How are Griffith and Sutton doing?'

'The prisoners of war are doing fine.'

'They're not prisoners of war, they're fucking hostages, so let's cut the horse-shit.'

McGee chuckled. 'Sure, you're a sharp one,

Barker. You can call them what you like, but we've got them and that's all that matters.' Barker didn't reply. There was a very long silence. 'So,' McGee said eventually, 'I take it you know our bomb works and we can get down to brass tacks.'

'It might work and it might not,' Barker replied. 'We want proof that you have it.'

'Eagle 3 was your proof.'

'That blast didn't come from an A-bomb, so don't pretend otherwise.'

'It doesn't matter,' McGee said. 'It was proof of our intentions. Proof that we could smuggle a bomb on board and that we mean what we say. You know we're not bluffing, Barker. Sure you're shit-scared and sweatin'. If you really want proof, try to take back this rig or simply refuse to meet our demands. You know what would happen then. If our bomb goes off, you're finished. It'll wipe out Beryl, devastate half of the Forties, and destroy the main pipeline to the refineries. That's over half of Britain's oil. We'll wipe the North Sea off the map. Think about that if you've got any idea that we're trying to bluff you.'

The radio shack was quiet but for the crackling static. It was growing dark outside and they heard the sea washing around the rig. Resting his chin in his hands, Barker stared blankly at the radio. He seemed pale and the shadows fell over him, rendering him ghostlike.

'What do you want?' he asked.

'The Prime Minister,' McGee replied.

'You want me to let you talk to the Prime Minister?'

'No,' McGee said. 'More than that.'

Barker almost stopped breathing. He leant back in his chair. After stretching his hands out on the table, he studied his fingernails. He didn't move for a long time and there was no sound from the radio. Barker finally sat forward again to speak into the microphone.

'You mean in person?' he asked.

'Ackaye. I mean in person.'

'And where do you plan to have this great meeting?'

'On Charlie 2,' McGee said.

Masters clenched his fists. He was thinking of the SBS assault squadrons presently on hold at the RM Commando base at Achnacarry. He was frustrated because he desperately wanted to call them out to deal with the terrorists, though that didn't seem likely. Opening his clenched fists, he glanced through the window. Shadows swooped across the sea. He saw the afternoon becoming evening, heard the wind, felt the deepening cold.

'You're kidding,' Barker said.

'Sure, I'm not,' McGee replied.

'You know we'd never fly the PM over there.'

'Sure, you've no choice,' McGee said.

Barker listened to the static like a man in a trance. The demands were impossible. The alternative was unthinkable. He glanced despairingly at Masters and Turner, then tried as best he could to fill the silence.

'I can't do that,' he said.

'You're going to have to,' McGee replied. 'I want the Prime Minister. I want him here by 1900 hours. Fifteen minutes after that, if he isn't here, I'll set the bomb off.'

'You'll go up with it,' Barker reminded him.

'You've already said that,' McGee responded. 'And I'm saying again, we don't mind. We're all committed to taking this to the limit if necessary. We're prepared to die for it.'

'Why do you want the Prime Minister?'

'I want to give him our demands.'

'Why not let me pass them on?'

'I want him as collateral.'

'Collateral?'

'That's right, Barker, our collateral. We need a guarantee as big as our demands, so we want the Prime Minister.'

'What the hell are you trying to pull, McGee? I want to know your demands.'

'You won't be told,' McGee said. 'I'll only inform the Prime Minister. He's the only man who's got the authority to get us what we want.'

'You might kill him,' Barker said.

'Ackaye, I might do that.'

'Then you know we can't possibly agree.'

'Sure, you will. You've no choice.'

Barker broke all the rules by lighting a cigarette. He inhaled and leant back in the chair and gazed up at the ceiling. Masters studied his face, which seemed thin and very pale. There were beads of sweat shining on his forehead, just beneath the hairline. It was quiet in the module, and they were all aware of the murmuring sea. Turner tugged at his beard and glanced at Masters, shook his head and looked down again. The tool-pusher remained standing, opening and shutting his large hands. Barker sat up, leant forward again, and looked straight at the radio.

'No arguments,' McGee said. 'No delays and no tricks. If anything comes anywhere near this rig, the whole thing'll go up in smoke. We want the Prime Minister. We want him at 1900 hours. We want him to arrive by helicopter with no cops or soldiers. You and Masters can come with him. I want Masters to fly the chopper. If we find another pilot on board, he'll be executed. You'll land at 1900 hours. We'll give you fifteen minutes' leeway. If you're not here by 1915 we'll blow the whole rig to hell.'

'I refuse,' Barker said.

'You can't refuse and you know it.'

'I won't do it.'

'I don't care,' McGee said. 'Sure, it's your choice, boyo.'

Barker opened his mouth to speak, but the line went dead on him. He sank back in the chair and fumbled for another cigarette.

'Jesus Christ,' he said quietly.

Masters looked out of the window at the darkening sea. Bravo 1 wasn't drilling, but he could hear the isolated roar of a fork-lift, the shouting of men. The radio continued crackling, though Charlie 2 was not receiving. Barker sat before the radio and stared at it while smoking his cigarette. Masters studied him and then looked at Turner.

'We can't,' Turner said. 'It's out of the question. We can't possibly give this news to the PM. It's too much to ask.'

'What else is there?' Barker asked him. 'The decision isn't ours to make. We can't take a chance on that bomb. We'll have to let *him* decide.'

'Let's go,' Masters said.

8

Each man in the boardroom looked about him as if suffering from shock. The news seemed so preposterous that they couldn't quite take it in, but gradually, in the grim silence following Turner's level recital, the awful reality sank in. Sir Reginald McMillan glanced at the Prime Minister, but could not meet his gaze. The PM's bright-blue gaze swept the table, then returned to the general supervisor.

'Well,' the PM said, 'that's quite a tale.'

'Yes, sir, I'm afraid so.'

'Nineteen hundred hours?'

'Yes, Prime Minister . . .'

'Then we have ninety minutes.'

Turner glanced at Masters and Barker. They were standing at the head of the long table, their eyes wandering back and forth. Sir Reginald glanced at Dalton. The American was smoking a cigarette and studying the others around the table with a steady, unblinking gaze. His eyes finally came to rest on the Prime Minister, whose bulky frame filled the chair. The PM was flicking the ash off his cigar and looking up at Turner.

'You can't do it,' Sir Reginald said. 'We can't let you go over there. We can't hand the Prime Minister of the United Kingdom to a bunch of murderous terrorists. It's completely out of the question.'

'I agree,' Dalton said. 'The request is just crazy. I'm all for trying to meet their demands, but I stop short at this.'

'Ludicrous,' Sir Reginald said. 'They must be utterly insane. I simply won't accept this.'

The PM leant forward in his chair. His florid, fleshy, stubborn face held a shrewd native cunning.

'Yes,' he said, 'it *is* ludicrous. That's *exactly* what it is. Now, what *I* want to know is how it happened. That really does interest me.' He turned his blue eyes on Barker, picked up his cigar, inhaled and blew the smoke into the air, then sat back and waited.

'It seems irrelevant . . .' Sir Reginald began defensively.

'It's not irrelevant,' the PM told him.

'Correct,' Dalton said. 'It's not irrelevant. It's a goddamn disgrace!'

The PM looked at Barker. 'So? I'm being asked to fly out to that rig and I want to know why.'

Barker sighed and shrugged his shoulders in defeat. 'Well,' he confessed, 'it seems we simply hired them as legitimate workers. We've been doing so for a long time.'

There was silence in the boardroom. Sir Reginald kept his head down. The PM breathed evenly in his chair and kept his eyes fixed on Barker. 'You *hired* them?' he asked.

'So it seems, sir. They signed up just like all the others and were shipped out the normal way.'

'Sixty terrorists,' the PM said.

'Yes, sir, that's the figure.'

'You're trying to tell me you signed on sixty terrorists without checking them out?'

'Not all at once, sir. They signed on over eighteen months. They came out of the dole queues and factories just like all the others.'

'I appreciate that, Mr Barker. I'm well aware of that fact. What I want to know is how a terrorist can get a job on an oil rig.'

'You don't check them out?' Dalton asked.

'No, we don't,' Barker confessed. 'There are so many unemployed, we don't bother checking credentials, so we don't know too much about their past.'

'This is incredible,' the PM said. 'It's utterly scandalous. Any fool, any madman can get a job on the oil rigs.'

'It's not *that* bad,' Sir Reginald said.

'It's bloody scandalous,' the PM told him. 'These

oil rigs are the life-blood of this country and you don't check who works on them.'

'I didn't realize,' Sir Reginald said. 'I must say, it *is* appalling. I shall, of course, order an investigation and demand a complete report.'

'It's Barker's bag,' Dalton said. 'He's in charge of security. I'd like to know how the hell he got his job if this is in any way typical.'

'I won't take that,' Barker said. 'I don't work in the employment office. My job is security on the rigs. I can't check out who's being hired.'

'So no one does,' Dalton said.

'I've been wanting checks for years,' Barker said, glancing at Sir Reginald. 'An inspection of my files will confirm that. My requests were denied.'

The PM glared at Sir Reginald. 'This is scandalous,' he repeated. 'You won't let the government touch the oilfields and this is what happens.'

They all glared at one another. The air was smoky and stank of brandy. Through the windows they could see the falling darkness, the lights winking on.

'Eightly minutes,' Masters said. 'We have exactly eighty minutes. I think we should be talking about Charlie 2. I think we'll have to decide.'

They all stared at Masters, surprised. The silence lasted a long time. 'Just who the hell *are* you?' Dalton finally asked him. 'And don't try telling us you're just a tool-pusher. That wouldn't get you into this boardroom with Messrs Turner and Barker. You're security, aren't you?'

Masters glanced from Barker to Turner, not sure what to say. Turner coughed into his fist and then reluctantly confessed: 'This man is a sergeant with the SBS – the Special Boat Squadron of the Royal Marine Commando. The SBS and the SAS have been given certain responsibilities regarding security in the oilfields. Sergeant Masters, though a former tool-pusher, is presently here on behalf of the SBS, acting under cover.'

There was another long silence while everyone took this in. The PM, who was furious, fought to control himself, though he couldn't help glaring at Sir Reginald. The latter's hands were folded in his lap and he kept staring at them. Eventually, when the tension became unbearable, the PM cleared his throat and said: 'This is neither the time nor the place to ask why I wasn't informed about this . . .'

'Neither was I,' Dalton interjected.

'And nor was I,' the Under-Secretary added.

'. . . though the matter will certainly not be forgotten,' the PM continued icily. 'But for now, given the urgency of our situation, let us stick to the issue in hand. And regarding that, as our SBS sergeant has informed us, we have to decide.'

'Decide what?' Sir Reginald asked, feigning outrage to cover his embarrassment. 'There's simply nothing *to* decide. Our Prime Minister isn't going on that rig and that's all there is to it.'

'I agree,' Dalton said.

'They have an A-bomb,' Masters reminded them.

'Correction,' Dalton said. 'We don't know that. We don't know that they have it.' He turned to the PM. 'We'll recapture the rig. We've no choice but to try it. We can't let you go to the terrorists. We don't know their intentions.'

'And the bomb?' the Under-Secretary asked. 'What happens about that? They've said they'll set it off if we attack. They might actually do so.'

'I think they would,' Masters said. 'I'm pretty certain they would. I don't think they'd be shy.'

The PM rubbed his forehead, stubbed out his cigar, clasped his hands under his chin, then gazed left and right. He avoided Sir Reginald, looked carefully at Masters, and finally his gaze came to rest on Dalton, who was pursing his lips.

'We're still assuming they have that bomb,' the American said. 'However, the fact that they had a photograph and a workable design doesn't mean they've managed to make the thing.'

'That's true,' Sir Reginald said. 'It seems a bit far-fetched to me. I don't think it's all that easy for amateurs to make an A-bomb. I find it hard to accept.'

'It's been known, sir,' Masters said. 'Our onshore men think it's possible. They say the materials can be bought on the open market and that the making of the actual bomb is relatively easy.'

'That's preposterous!' Sir Reginald snapped.

'No, it's not,' Dalton said. 'There's kids making them in their backyards in the States. They're pretty crude, but they would work.'

'It would help if we had proof,' Masters said. 'And Andrew Blackburn of our onshore security is trying to find it.'

'*He'll* be lucky,' Sir Reginald said.

The emergency telephone rang. Every head in the room turned towards Barker as he picked it up. There was a tense, lingering silence. Barker covered one ear. He nodded and then lowered the phone and looked at each man in turn.

'It's Blackburn,' he told them. 'They're putting him through now. I think he should talk on the open line to let us all hear this.'

'I don't think . . .' Sir Reginald began.

'I certainly do,' the PM interjected. 'I think we should *all* be kept informed from this moment on.'

Barker glanced at Sir Reginald. The Chairman nodded reluctantly. Barker pressed a button on the telephone and they all heard a soft, hissing sound.

'Blackburn?'

'Yes, Barker. We've managed to check out this McGee. It wasn't very difficult at all. He didn't cover his tracks.'

'Good,' Barker said. 'Go ahead.'

'Is this line scrambled?'

'Yes, Andy, go on.'

'Good. I think it's all pretty dodgy.'

Blackburn was silent for a moment, obviously checking his notes. Those waiting studied the speakers on the boardroom walls, most too breathless to speak.

'McGee lived in a boarding house,' Blackburn said eventually. 'In George Street in Aberdeen. He's been using the same place for the past two years, every time he's on shore. A pretty normal boarding house. A typical rig worker's place. McGee used to have a lot of friends in, but apart from that the landlord had no complaints. We searched his room. He hadn't attempted to hide anything. The search revealed correspondence between himself and various known members of the IRA. McGee was clearly quite high up. The correspondence covered a lot. Plans for bombings and assassinations and hijackings, most of which, as the records now reveal, were accomplished successfully.'

Sir Reginald coughed into his fist. The PM glared at him. Sir Reginald offered a smile that was rejected, so he studied the floor.

'Also found,' Blackburn continued, 'was a notebook with some odd addresses, including one for a closed-down car repair place. I only mention this because it ties in with the fact that we also found invoices from various specialist libraries and bookshops, all of which were unusual. Included were the National Technical Information Service of the US Department of Commerce; the US Atomic Energy Commission; the Science Reference Library in Chancery Lane, London; and the Office of Technical Services. A subsequent search of the closed repair shop revealed various books – all openly available from the sources I've just named and all filled with unclassified and declassified – but extremely dangerous – information. Among these books were both volumes of *The Plutonium Handbook*; another book called *The Science of High Explosives* – this one written by Melvin Cook, Professor of Metallurgy and director of the Explosives Research Group of the University of Utah – and, finally, the *Source Book on Atomic Energy* and the *Los Alamos Primer*. This last book consists of notes made during the production of the first A-bomb in Los Alamos, New Mexico, and is published openly by the US Atomic Energy Commission.'

'Did you say "published openly"?' Sir Reginald asked.

'That's right,' Blackburn replied, failing to use the proper form of address because he didn't know to whom he was talking. 'These are treated as information libraries. This information, which our own experts have confirmed is extremely dangerous, is, as I said, either unclassified or declassified and therefore freely available to the general public. You just walk in and pay for the books and that's all there is to it.'

'That's scandalous!' Sir Reginald exclaimed.

The PM glared at him. Embarrassed, Sir Reginald coughed noisily again and gazed at the speakers.

'Anyway,' Blackburn continued, 'this is particularly interesting. Also found in that supposedly closed workshop were traces of plutonium oxide – which I'm told can be converted easily into concentrated plutonium nitrate; an electrical induction furnace; a sealed glove-box of the type used to avoid contamination; high-temperature crucibles; hydrofluoric acid, oxalic acid, metallic calcium, crystalline iodine, quartz glassware, and a cylinder of argon and nitric acid – all available on the open market; all ingredients for a workable plutonium bomb.'

Blackburn let his words sink in. None of the men in the boardroom spoke. Finally, after what seemed like a long time, Barker asked him a question.

'What does all this mean?' he said. 'That they could make it?'

'Yes,' replied Blackburn. 'All the information needed to put those materials together into a working bomb can be found in the books I've just named – and the bomb could be made in a car workshop or something even less grand. According to our lab boys, any particularly complicated calculations could be done simply by using hired computer time with any legitimate computer firm. The computer operator, probably innocent, would be shown nothing other than a set of partial differential equations and a written request for a particular programme to be run. He or she therefore wouldn't have a clue what it was for. Also, suitable explosive lenses are now commercially available just about anywhere; and the initiator and other materials can be bought over the counter from any firm supplying university labs. In short, your terrorists appear to have made their plutonium bomb.'

Dalton gave a low whistle. Turner wiped sweat from his brow. The PM was immobile, staring up at the loudspeakers as if not believing his ears. Masters looked at each man in turn and sensed the fear grow in all of them.

'OK,' Barker said. 'So they made their bomb. But could they test it without setting it off?'

'Dead easy,' Blackburn said. 'Piece of pie, really. They only have to test the detonating circuits for simultaneity – and the equipment for this is also available on the open market. Apart from ordinary metering equipment, it would consist of a double-beam oscilloscope with long-stay traces, a pulse-height analyser, and an accurate recording digital timer – all on sale commercially. My lab boys tell me that they've previously come across arming devices made from cooker timers and second-hand servo-motors; and that the detonation circuits can actually be linked to a device known to every telephone engineer – an arrangement that allows detonation of the bomb by phone on any line using STD codes. So they could have – and probably have – tested their bomb.'

Turner sat in a chair and covered his face with his hands. The PM watched him, then glanced at Sir Reginald, who seized this opportunity to wriggle out of his own guilt by launching an attack on the Under-Secretary.

'I can't believe it,' the Chairman said. 'I cannot believe my own ears. I am informed that the materials and the instructions for a workable atom bomb are freely available to the general public. I find this whole thing appalling.'

The Under-Secretary refused to rise to the bait.

'Any more?' Barker asked.

'A bit,' Blackburn said. 'We tried tracing the people detailed in McGee's notebook and we managed to find some. A few are in prison, others have disappeared, and a fair amount are working on the oil rigs. I assume that's your problem.'

Turner uncovered his face to look across at Sir Reginald, who was leaning back in his chair, staring up at the ceiling. He had almost stopped breathing.

'Yes,' Barker said, 'that's our problem. It's a very big problem. I'm classifying this whole item top secret and I want it to stay that way.'

'Right,' Blackburn said.

'Put a seal across it.'

'Will do,' Blackburn said. 'Have no fear. Is there anything else?'

'No, nothing else.'

'Best of luck,' Blackburn said.

The line went dead. Barker switched off the phone, turned away and stared into space, then shrugged his shoulders.

They all sat for a while in silence. The sea was a remote, rhythmic murmuring all around the platform. It was now dark outside and the platform's lights were blazing, throwing shadows across the tiered decks and reflecting off the antennae.

'So,' the Under-Secretary said. 'They probably have a working bomb. They may use it, but they may just be bluffing and there's one way to find out. Are we willing to take that risk? Can we afford to do so? All in all, I don't think we can risk it. There's too much at stake here.'

'And if we don't?' the PM asked. 'If we wait until seven-fifteen? What happens if we wait and the bomb goes off? Can we possibly live with that?'

'It's your life at stake, Prime Minister. We don't know what they want. Those men are assassins – they've killed before and they will again – and of all the political figures in this country, you're the biggest prize there is. I don't think you should do it. You shouldn't take that chance. I think we should recapture that rig before they set the bomb off.'

'That's impossible,' Masters said.

'Why?' the Under-Secretary asked.

'All the rigs have radar. That means we can't use boats. They've got cameras and sonic beams beneath the water, so we can't use submersibles. There's no way we can surprise them. It's out of the question. We either sit here and pray that they're bluffing or we do as they say.'

'I see,' the Under-Secretary said to the others around the table. 'Our SBS colleague wants to risk the Prime Minister. He's willing to risk our Prime Minister's life on a mere speculation.'

'They're not bluffing,' Masters insisted.

'We don't know that,' Sir Reginald said.

'So what if they're not bluffing?' the PM asked. 'I don't think we can risk that.'

'You're the head of the British government,' the Under-Secretary said. 'You can't give yourself up to the terrorists on the chance that they'll spare you.'

'Is there a choice?' the PM asked. 'I can't see that there is. A bomb like that will finish off the North Sea, not to mention the UK. So I *don't* think there's a choice. I side with Sergeant Masters. We'll just have to see what they want and hope it isn't my neck.'

'Once you're there, there's not a thing we can do,' the Under-Secretary said, 'and they can do what they want. They could kill you and *still* set the bomb off – or set it off while you're on the rig.'

'True enough,' Masters said, 'but we still don't have a choice. And at least, if we can get on that rig, we have the chance to do something.'

'*Do* something, Sergeant?'

'That's right, sir – do something. It's a long shot, but at least we'll be aboard and that counts for something. I might be able to get away. I don't know how, but it's possible. I might be able to disappear long enough to find out where the bomb is. If I do, I can disarm it. I know enough about those things to do that. I can ensure that it won't work and then we'll take it from there.'

'They'll kill you,' Dalton said.

'At least they won't have their bomb. And if they don't have their bomb, then the only thing they have is the rig.'

'They'll kill you,' Dalton insisted. 'You *and* the Prime Minister. If you take their bomb apart, they're going to kill you. I'm certain of that.'

'It's our only chance,' Masters said. 'Our only possible hope. It's a long shot, but it's the only one we've got, so we might as well take it.'

'It's suicide,' the Under-Secretary insisted. 'There's no other word for it.'

'It's a chance,' Masters said.

The PM stared at him. It was a hard and searching look. His penetrating blue eyes were set in a rough worker's face. He saw that Masters was looking back. There was no sign of intimidation. He saw intelligence and a growing frustration and a fierce, controlled anger. There was no other option. While they talked the bomb was ticking away and the future was shrinking. The PM didn't like it. He didn't really want to do it. He studied Masters and wondered what would happen if they sat it out. The bomb might go off. The oilfields would be destroyed. His own future and the future of Britain would go down with the rigs. There could be no doubt about it. The PM studied the SBS sergeant and saw his one hope on earth. 'We've no choice,' he said.

9

The black sky was all around them. Below was nothing but darkness. The RN Dragonfly helicopter rose and fell on the wind as it headed for the Beryl Field, powered by its single Pratt & Whitney R-985 450-hp engine. Masters was at the controls with Barker beside him. The Prime Minister, seated close behind them, coughed lightly to clear his throat.

Masters glanced down at the sea and saw a dark, vitreous void. He didn't like to look down – it was the black void of a dream. They were fifteen hundred feet above the sea but couldn't see a thing. Masters felt very strange, slightly high, his nerves tingling. Excitement was mixed up with his natural fear and clinging sense of disbelief.

He was a Royal Marine Commando, a member of the SBS, trained rigorously at the Amphibious School of the Royal Marines at Eastney and elsewhere in a remarkably wide variety of specialist activities, including offensive demolitions, close-quarter combat (CQB), firing rifles and automatic weapons from the hip, stalking, fighting in densely wooded country and on the streets, abseiling, navigation, assault-opposed landings, elementary bridging, the use of assault boats and scaling ladders, tactical manoeuvres involving endurance, living on concentrated rations, ambushes, night operations, general boating, parachuting and flying single-pilot aircraft and helicopters – all that and he was still nervous, not because of the nature of this operation, but because he was now in charge of the fate of the British Prime Minister.

Luckily, if he survived this op, he would no longer be alone. Just before flying from Bravo 1 with the PM, he had been ordered by the latter to obtain proper authorization from his CO to make this flight and engage with the terrorists. Shocked by what he had been told, the CO, Lieutenant-Colonel Ben Edwards, had insisted on flying out to Bravo 1 to confer with the others in the boardroom and personally supervise all further SBS activity in the matter, including, if necessary, a full rescue assault against Charlie 2. On hold with his SBS squadron in the old Commando Basic Training Centre at Achnacarry, near the foot of Ben Nevis, Lieutenant-Colonel Edwards had decided to fly with one of his most experienced officers, Captain Rudolph 'Rudy' Pancroft, to Bravo 1 even as Masters was *en route* to Charlie 2. By the time Masters returned from Charlie 2 – if he returned – his two superiors would be relocated on Bravo 1. This thought gave him some comfort.

Masters looked down again and saw blackness everywhere. There was no moon, but he did see the clouds as deeper stains on the darkness. He shivered a little, his excitement warring with fear, as the Dragonfly dropped into an air pocket, shook violently, then picked up speed again and flew on.

'Are we close?' the PM asked.

'Yes, Prime Minister,' Masters replied. 'We should be seeing their lights any minute now. We'll be descending soon.'

'What time is it?'

'Eighteen-fifty hours,' Barker informed him.

'Ten minutes,' the Prime Minister said. 'I trust they'll be amenable now.'

Masters didn't reply. His brain was racing with possibilities. He wondered where he would be held, where the bomb was hidden, if he could make his escape and stay out of sight long enough. It wouldn't take long to dismantle; the time spent would be in locating it. He had to elude his captors long enough to find and destroy the bomb. And what if he succeeded? Would that help in the long run? He tried to think of a way of escaping but couldn't come up with one. After all, he had the Prime Minister and Barker to think about as well. He couldn't simply disarm the bomb and run away, leaving them trapped with the terrorists. His mind was racing, yet his eyes scanned the dark sky systematically. Looking down, he saw distant, winking lights and knew they were close.

'That's it,' Barker hissed.

'Yeah, I can see it.'

'I feel trapped,' Barker said. 'Utterly useless. What can we do down there?'

Masters looked ahead and saw the distant lights approaching, pinpoints growing bigger in the darkness to become stars in space, then lamps floating on high. There was something chilling in that sight, something unreal and frightening. Suddenly, he felt all alone, floating free in the cosmos. He blinked and swallowed, torn between dread and excitement, then gave in to a cold, competitive rage against the men on that rig. He had to beat them somehow, deprive them of victory. His own future, and that of his country, both hung in the balance.

'I'm starting the descent now,' he said.

'I'm glad,' the PM replied gamely. 'I want to get this over and done with. I don't like not knowing.'

The distant lights were approaching rapidly. Moonlight fell on the water. The Dragonfly, shaking a little, dropped lower and Masters saw Charlie 2. It was a pyramid of lights that rendered the rig invisible. The lights seemed to be floating in the dark sky above the moon's reflection in the water.

That water was almost black – a bottomless well. The lights of Charlie 2 shone above it, danced and leapt in the lapping waves. Masters tried to concentrate, taking the helicopter lower. He had a vision of the lights of Manhattan, sweeping out, soaring skywards. It was a beautiful sight that made him catch his breath. He looked down and saw the silhouetted derricks, the black mat of the platform.

'There they are,' he said. 'The bastards are waiting down there for us. Now let's find out what's happening.'

He turned the Dragonfly around and started descending towards the rig, heading for the circle of lights on the edge of the platform. Now he could see the whole rig, the towering derricks and tiered modules, a patchwork of shadow and light, stark black and white brilliance. There were dots in that mosaic, moving back and forth, gradually taking shape and becoming the human beings surrounding the landing pad. The Dragonfly shuddered as it dropped below the lights. Far below, beneath the illuminated landing pad, was the dark, surging sea. The helicopter descended vertically until the derricks towered above it. Dropping lower, it touched lightly on the deck and finally came to a halt.

Masters switched off the engine and waited patiently until the props had stopped rotating and the slipstream had subsided.

'Here we go,' Barker said.

The men moving in on all sides were wearing overalls and were armed with 5.56mm Heckler & Koch MP5 sub-machine-guns, 7.6mm Kalashnikov AK47 semi-automatic assault rifles, and a variety of handguns, including the 9mm Glock 17 semi-automatic and the .455-inch Webley Mark 6. The lights washed across their faces, rendering them ghostly white and featureless. They closed in, surrounding the Dragonfly, as Masters moved towards the door. The PM hesitated when he saw those floodlit faces. Beyond them were the blazing lights of the derricks and the stark, jet-black shadows.

Masters smiled reassuringly at the PM, then unlocked the door. After sliding the door open, he threw out the short ladder and made his way down, followed by Barker. A cold air rushed into the helicopter as the PM stood up, bit his lower lip, then moved to the exit and stared down at the brightly lit landing pad. The terrorists were keeping Masters and Barker covered, but otherwise they seemed calm. The PM took a deep breath and made his way down the ladder until he stood between Masters and Barker.

'So,' Masters asked, 'where's McGee?'

One of the terrorists stepped forward and grabbed Masters by the shoulder, jerked him around, threw him against the side of the helicopter and then roughly kicked his legs apart. Masters offered no resistance. The terrorist ran his hands up and down the SBS man's body, then stepped back and motioned to Barker.

'Your turn,' he said.

Barker faced the Dragonfly, putting his hands above his head and spreading his legs. The terrorist frisked him expertly, then stepped back and nodded at the Prime Minister.

'You, too,' he said quietly.

The PM straightened his broad shoulders and stared straight at the terrorist. 'I am the Prime Minister of the United Kingdom,' he declared. 'I do not carry weapons.'

The terrorist raised his MP5 sub-machine-gun and aimed it at the PM. 'I don't give a fuck,' the terrorist said. 'Put your hands on that chopper.'

The PM bristled, but did as he was told. The terrorist frisked him and then stepped away, saying: 'Right, turn around.' The three men did as they were told, facing the circle of armed terrorists. The wind moaned and stark shadows formed a web on the steel of the platform.

'Where's McGee?' Masters asked again.

'In the radio shack,' replied the terrorist who had frisked them.

'I know where it is,' Masters said. 'Are we going there now?'

'Right now. After you.'

The terrorist motioned with his MP5, the surrounding men parted to form a pathway, and Masters, followed by the PM and Barker, headed for the catwalk. The PM glanced left and right and saw the weapons pointing at him. He felt a tension that wasn't quite fear – more a heightened awareness. Some armed terrorists went on ahead while others fell in behind. Masters mounted the catwalk, Barker close behind, and then the PM also stepped forward and felt the blast of an icy wind. Following Barker across the catwalk, he glanced down and felt dizzy. The surging sea way below was a dark pit flecked with silvery lights. The PM took a deep breath and gripped the railing tighter. There was nothing on either side but the sea and the sky, both black, both offering lonesome sounds: splashing water, the moaning wind. The PM stopped once. He was prodded with a gun barrel. Advancing again, he walked carefully down the catwalk, eventually finding himself standing on the main deck, beside Masters and Barker.

'Keep going,' the leading terrorist said. 'You're not here for the scenery.'

The gunmen formed a circle around them as they crossed the main deck. There were more terrorists standing along the modules, looking on with great interest, some laughing, others shouting derisory remarks. The PM kept his dignity, not responding in any way, following the others past huge oil tanks and derricks, under cranes and catwalks. The deck was slippery under foot, filmed with mud and oil, and they walked either through the dazzling brilliance of the floodlights or through a stark, blinding blackness. It was very quiet here. The drilling floor had been silenced. They heard the wind, the sea, their boots banging on metal.

They came to a steel ladder leading up to another deck. The terrorists in front climbed up, Masters and Barker followed, and then the PM, breathing heavily. It was a vertical climb and he wasn't used to such exercise; when he reached the top he found himself gasping, felt the strain in his muscles. Barker was grinning at him, at once amused and admiring. Masters was intently studying their surroundings, fixing them in his memory. Following the SBS man's gaze, the PM saw the radio shack. The front door was open, light was flooding out, and a man was silhouetted in the doorway, surrounded by armed guards.

'Is that McGee?' the PM asked.

'Yes,' Masters replied.

'Obviously he has a flair for theatrics,' the PM said.

They walked across the deck and stepped into the light. McGee, unarmed, was in the doorway, a grin on his face.

'Have you come?' he said to Masters, using that oddity of speech peculiar to Ulster.

'Yes. Here we are.'

'Did I surprise you?'

'Yes, McGee, you surprised me. I would never have guessed.'

McGee's grin was not good-humoured. His brown eyes, bright and hard, turned from Masters to Barker to finally settle on the PM, whom he studied for some time. The PM was unflinching. McGee turned away and motioned the three men inside. Brushing past him, they entered the radio shack, which was small, bright and sweltering. McGee stepped in after them, flanked by two armed guards. One of them closed the door, the other moved up beside him, and both of them levelled their MP5s at the three visitors. McGee grinned, sat down by the radio and looked up at his hostages.

'Sure, I thought I'd make this radio shack my HQ,' he explained. 'Particularly when we'd so much to talk about.'

No one smiled. 'All right,' Barker said. 'You've got us here, so just tell us one thing. Is there really a bomb?'

'Ackaye,' McGee replied.

'Where?'

'Where do you think? Inside one of the pontoon legs – just like the first one.'

'Which leg?' Masters asked.

'Don't be daft, Tone. Do you think I'd be

dumb enough to tell you? Ask me something else, like.'

'Would you really use it?' the PM asked.

'Ackaye, Prime Minister.'

'You must be mad,' Barker told him.

'No, I'm not. And you damn well know it.'

McGee stopped grinning, looked at each of them in turn, then settled his gaze on Masters.

'Tell us about the bomb,' Masters said.

'Sure, Tone, why not?' McGee grinned again. 'It's about the size of a tea chest and weighs . . .'

'We already know that,' Masters interrupted.

'Right,' McGee said, grinning even more broadly, though with no sign of humour. 'It was shipped in in separate parts in various supply crates, over a period of time, and the parts were hidden in the rig's regular storage space. A lot of my men were on the night shift and often had to check the pontoon legs; so bit by bit they took the parts down into the pontoon leg and gradually reassembled the bomb down there. It's now resting on a girder halfway down – and it's all primed to go.'

He grinned at the three of them. They all looked at him in silence. The floor was undulating from side to side, very slowly, hypnotically. Eventually the PM coughed into his fist, clearing his throat.

'What are your demands?' he asked quietly.

'I speak for the IRA,' McGee responded portentously. 'I want you to understand that. These demands are on behalf of the Irish . . .'

'I don't wish to hear your nonsense,' the PM snapped. 'I just want your demands.'

'We want one million pounds sterling. Then we want four of our men out of the Maze prison. It's as simple as that.'

'What men?' the PM asked.

'You mean you agree to the money?'

'I haven't said that,' the PM replied firmly. 'Now who are these men?'

'Seamus McGrath, John Houlihan, Kevin Trainor and Shaun McGurk – the four best men we've got.'

'That's rather a large demand,' the PM said after a lengthy pause. 'I seriously doubt that I could order their release.'

'Sure you can, Prime Minister. You can dream up an excuse. They're political prisoners, there's already doubt that you can hold them long, but we want them to be pardoned and set free before this week's out. We won't settle for less.'

'That's impossible,' the PM said.

'Sure, nothing's impossible, Prime Minister. We don't care how you explain it to the public; we just want them pardoned.'

'I can't do it,' the PM said.

'Yes, you can,' McGee insisted. 'They're in the

Maze awaiting trial, their guilt hasn't been proven yet, so you can say that the evidence against them was all circumstantial and wouldn't have held up in court.'

'That will make fools of our intelligence people.'

'That's part of our general plan.'

'And the million pounds? You want us to give you a million pounds so you can finance more terror?'

'Ackaye, that's right, Prime Minister. That's just what we want, like.'

The PM stared at him with cold rage in his eyes, then scratched his chin and studied the floor, clearly deep in thought. Eventually raising his eyes again, he said: 'Then what? You've already done all the damage you can. I can't see us recovering from the public knowledge that all this has happened.'

'That's correct,' Barker interjected. 'You've done too much damage already. We'll lose international confidence when this gets out and that will finish the North Sea.'

'It won't be public,' McGee explained. 'It doesn't have to be known. Sure, if you give us what we want, we'll pull out and keep quiet about it. Then you people put out a statement. You say the loss of Eagle 3 was due to a serious earthquake on the seabed that caused damage as far away as Charlie 2. You say most of the crew on Charlie 2 were killed and will have to be replaced. Naturally, we'll be gone. You then bring the new crew in. They'll take over without knowing what's gone on – nor will anyone else.'

'To your advantage,' the PM said.

'Ackaye, Prime Minister. Sure we'll stay quiet as long as our men stay out of the Maze. We'll only talk if you try to drag them back in or otherwise harm them.'

The PM was thoughtful, pursing his lips and tapping his chin with his fingertips as the hut swayed from side to side.

Eventually, to break the silence, Robert Barker said: 'So what if we agree? What guarantee do we have that the Prime Minister will then be released and that the bomb won't be set off?'

'Now why would we do that? We'd be cutting our own throats. Why destroy British oilfields and kill the Prime Minister, turning public sympathy against us, when we've got everything we need with minimum damage? We rely on public support as much as you do and we don't want to lose it.'

'So why demand the PM's presence here in the first place?'

'Because there's something I have to tell you in his presence – and you're not going to like it.' He glanced at each of them in turn, grim-faced now. After checking the guard by the door, he turned back to them. 'The IRA couldn't have financed an operation this big on its own. No, we were approached by the spokesman for some overseas backers who wanted us to assassinate the Prime Minister.' McGee's thin smile at this point was not returned by the PM. 'We only had one meeting with this single representative and he didn't say who the others were. He only described them as a group with unlimited funds. But since he specifically wanted the assassination to take place during the PM's visit to the oilfields, I think it's safe to assume that they've some interests here.'

Masters felt a sudden chill sliding down his spine. He was shocked by this fresh revelation, the thickening plot, and felt that he, an SBS commando, a good marine, was out of his depths in this murky world of conspiracy.

'This unknown group,' McGee continued, 'wanted the assassination to look like the act of a local terrorist group. For reasons not explained they didn't want it to be connected to anyone outside the United Kingdom. They wanted us to do the job. We also had to take the blame. In return, they would finance the hijack operation and pay a separate fee of two million pounds.'

Barker glanced at his granite-faced Prime Minister, then lowered his gaze to the floor. Masters knew he was shocked.

'As I said before,' McGee continued, 'it's not in our interest to lose public sympathy by assassinating the Prime Minister – but we needed the money and we *did* want our men out of the Maze.

So we accepted the job, receiving full finance for the hijack and with the first half of the two million to be paid to our representatives in Aberdeen the minute you all stepped aboard this rig. The other million was to be paid when we killed the Prime Minister.'

'I don't get it,' Barker said. 'How would these men, your backers, know that the Prime Minister had boarded this rig? Would they take your word for it?'

'Of course not. They'd know because one of them – and I honestly don't know who – is one of the men who took part in your conference back on Bravo 1. He'll know the Prime Minister's here. He'll know everything that's happened. He'll be contacting the mainland right now, to arrange for the first million to be handed over. When my man rings to say that's been done, I'm to kill the Prime Minister . . . begging your pardon, sir!'

The PM responded with a flat gaze. 'But you won't kill me,' he said.

'No,' McGee replied. 'And I've already told you why. I don't know who these men are, but alienating the British public is something we wouldn't do for their benefit. They offered two million pounds. We want you to offer more. Their first million plus your million makes two million – the original fee – but we also want our men out of the Maze and that's really the capper.'

There was silence for a long time while they tried to digest the facts. Masters, Barker and the PM were all thinking of Bravo 1 and the unknown traitor in their midst. Which one of them was it? What was his motivation? Who on earth could have set all this up while pretending to be one of their own? Barker looked stunned and drained. Masters was still and self-contained. The Prime Minister, by contrast, was shocked and outraged, his icy-blue eyes bright with a burning anger.

'I won't agree,' he said harshly. 'The price is too high. I will not release your murderous friends from the Maze just to watch them organize more terrorism. Nor will I give you the money. I won't finance the IRA. To capitulate will merely be a sign that you can get away with this again. No, I won't do it. Nothing you say will make me do it. There are limits and I think you've just reached them. You won't go any further.'

'That I will,' McGee promised.

'I don't think so, McGee. You said yourself that you depend on public opinion, so I don't think you'll risk turning it against you. You won't do what you're threatening.'

The second he finished speaking, he realized how wrong he was. He looked into the growing rage in McGee's eyes and saw the truth of fanaticism. McGee was pushing his chair back, standing up, his eyes widening. He grabbed the PM by the collar to tug him forward and breathe right in his face.

'Sure, I'll do it,' McGee snapped. 'Believe me, mister, I'll do it! I'll do anything that puts you bastards down, even if I go with you!' He pushed the PM aside, snatched a pistol from the table, then violently kicked the door open and stepped out of the hut. 'Bring the bastards out here!' he bawled.

One of the guards grabbed the PM and threw him out through the door. When he nodded curtly at Masters and Barker, both men left the radio shack, stepping into the light beaming out from the doorway and further dazzled by the lights shining down from the derricks and modules. Temporarily blinded, they blinked and then saw the two survivors: Griffith and Sutton, the geologist and the driller, both on their hands and knees on the deck, surrounded by gunmen. Sutton had been badly beaten; his face was bruised and he was weeping. Griffith, kneeling beside him, was untouched, but his eyes shone with fear.

McGee didn't waste any time. He grabbed Griffith by the hair, jerked his head back, placed the barrel of the pistol against his head and then glanced around wildly at the PM. The latter tried to step forward, but two of the guards stopped him, then twisted his arms behind his back and held him there while he looked on in horror.

'No!' the PM cried out. 'No! For God's sake, you can't . . .'

His voice was cut off by the gunshot. Griffith's head exploded. His body jerked like a puppet on a string and then collapsed to the deck.

'Do you believe me?' McGee hissed.

He spun around and grabbed Sutton and jerked his head back. Sutton shrieked and the Prime Minister cried 'No!' and then the gun fired again. Sutton convulsed and collapsed. His body shuddered and then was still. The blood dribbled from the shadows where his head was to touch the PM's boots. The Prime Minister started sagging, but the guards pulled him back up. He shook his head from side to side as if dazed, then started shaking all over. McGee walked up to him, his eyes bright and obsessed, and waved his gun in the PM's face as if wanting to hit him.

'Do you believe me?' he hissed again. 'Well? Is that enough for your conscience?'

The Prime Minister did not reply, but simply gasped and shook his head. Barker bit his lower lip and Masters clenched both his fists as the two bodies were thrown overboard. They didn't hear the splash: the sea was too far below. They glanced down and saw the blood on the deck, seeping out of the shadows. The PM shuddered and Barker bit his lip again. Masters opened his clenched fists and spread his fingers as he fought to control himself.

The huge derricks soared above him, their lights merging with the stars. Masters dropped his gaze only when he was prodded, none too gently, at gunpoint, back into the hut.

The PM was in a chair, covering his face with his hands, shuddering. Barker was standing beside him, clearly as shocked but trying to hide it. Masters, turning away in embarrassment, came face to face with McGee.

'You have one hour to decide,' McGee said, before slamming the door shut.

10

The Prime Minister raised his head and looked at them with shocked eyes. He shuddered and then controlled himself and sat up in the chair. Covering his face with his hands again, he took deep, even breaths, then removed his hands from his face, placed them lightly on his knees and stared at them as if praying for clemency.

'My fault,' he said softly. 'So stupid. God forgive me for that.'

'It wasn't your fault,' Masters said. 'I think he wanted to do it anyway. He wanted to put on a show and he used you for that.'

The PM shook his head. 'I can't believe it, Sergeant . . . Like animals . . . They were shot down like animals. One always thinks men can't do that.'

'They can do it,' Masters told him. 'They've been doing it for centuries. Let's forget it. Let's talk about something else. We've got one hour to stop it.'

'Stop it?' Barker said. 'How the hell can we stop

it? We're locked in and they won't let us out. We just say yes or no.'

'Wrong,' Masters said. 'McGee made one mistake. Of all the places on the rig to lock us up, he picked the wrong one.'

Barker looked sharply at him, then glanced around the radio shack. The single window had a solid metal covering which the terrorists had locked.

'We can get *out*?' Barker asked.

'That's right,' Masters said. 'But what happens then, I don't know.'

He glanced at the PM, who was still taking deep breaths. The PM's eyes were clearer now, and he seemed to be calming down.

'Are you all right, sir?' Masters asked.

'Yes, I'm all right. I don't feel good, but that can be lived with. Apart from that, I'm OK.'

'They forgot something,' Masters told him. 'They probably don't even know about it. This hut has a trapdoor in the floor, practically under your feet.'

The PM glanced down and saw nothing but solid steel. He looked between his legs, under the console, and saw a steel plate. It had an embedded handle.

'That's it,' Masters confirmed. 'It leads down to the drilling floor. This hut's above one corner of that floor, well away from the moonpool. The corner's packed with large crates, filled with spare parts and antennae. If anything goes wrong with the communications unit, the spare parts are passed up through the trapdoor. We can get down to that floor. The packing crates will give us cover. That corner of the floor rests on top of a pontoon leg and an exit door leads out to the catwalk. Ladders run down the pontoon legs – straight down to the sea. I know that there's a supply barge anchored beside the rig and since they always unload from this side that's where it'll be. We can climb down the pontoon leg. There'll be no one on the barge. If we go down the inside of the leg there's no way we'll be seen.'

'And once there?' Barker asked. 'What happens then? Do we just hide and wait?'

'No,' Masters said. 'We don't have to do that. The barges are towed out by small boats, so we'll take one of those. They're not fast, but they'll do. We'll have to time it pretty well. McGee's left the radio open to let us ring Bravo 1 because he thinks we can't get away anyhow. So we *will* ring Bravo 1. We'll ask for a helicopter to pick us up. It's not much, but it's something.'

'We can't just leave,' the PM said. 'I don't think we should do that.'

'The bomb,' Barker explained.

'That's right,' Masters said. 'We have to disarm the bomb and kill their radar and cameras. If we manage that, we can return. Launch an assault against the rig. With their cameras and sonic beams out of action, we can come under the sea and get to the rig before they see us. In short, we have to leave them paralysed until we come back.'

'It's impossible,' Barker said. 'It can't be done. We don't know where the bomb is.'

'I think I do,' Masters told him. 'McGee said a bit too much. He said the bomb was inside a pontoon leg – halfway down a pontoon leg.'

'You're going to search for it?' Barker asked.

'That's right,' Masters said. 'The support legs are hollow, they're laced with steel ladders, and if I don't find the bomb in the first leg, I'll climb through to the next.'

'You haven't time,' Barker said. 'The four main legs are a quarter of a mile apart. You haven't time to check all of them.'

'I won't have to,' Masters said. 'At least I might, but I doubt it. I think the bomb is on this side of the rig and probably right there below us. McGee's made this hut his base. He wants to be near the radio. I suspect he'd automatically place the bomb in the leg nearest to him. There's another reason for him to do that. The offloading is done this side. When McGee brought the bomb aboard, whether it was well hidden or not, I think he would have wanted it stored in the nearest available spot. The closest spot is beneath this hut; it's the first storage space you come to. Christ, come to think of it, he said the bomb was packed with some radio spares

– and all the radio spares are stored beneath this hut. That's where the bomb is – I'm almost certain of it. It's in the pontoon leg directly below us.'

Barker gave a low whistle. 'If you're right,' he said, 'that just leaves the radar and cameras. How the hell can you kill them?'

'I'm not sure,' Masters confessed. 'But if I cannibalize the plutonium bomb, I might be able to make some more modest explosives. I suspect the terrorist bomb is an implosion-type weapon, which means that the plutonium metal core is surrounded by a large quantity of ordinary, conventional explosive, such as dynamite.'

'*Sticks* of dynamite?' said Barker.

'Yes. And if it's that kind of bomb – and I think it has to be – I'll use the dynamite on the antennae and the drilling room.'

'You'll never get there,' Barker said. 'The terrorists are bound to see you.'

'I'm not sure that they will,' Masters replied. 'There are sixty terrorists aboard and they all arrived separately over the last eighteen months. They all worked with the regular crew and they all worked in shifts. Given the size of this rig and the nature of shift work, I think it's safe to assume that one half has never seen the other half. A lot are probably meeting for the first time. Some probably haven't even met yet. I'm in overalls and I look just like the rest, so they probably won't give me a second glance. True, McGee knows me and a lot of the men outside have seen me; but I think those men are all stationed on this deck, so if I can manage to keep out of McGee's way I'll have a fairly good chance.'

The SBS man's grey eyes shone with a hard, driving light as they focused steadily, relentlessly, on Barker. The Prime Minister was standing up. He wasn't shaking any more. The colour had returned to his face and he gave a small smile.

'I don't believe this,' he said.

Masters grinned. 'It's a long shot,' he confessed. 'But we don't really have another choice, so I think we should try it.'

'Yes,' the PM said, 'so do I.'

'There's no time,' Barker said. 'We've only fifty minutes left. That gives us time to get off this rig. There's no time for the rest of it.'

'You want to leave them with the bomb?'

'No, I don't. I just think fifty minutes is too short. There's no way you can do it.'

'If the bomb's below I can.'

'It might not be below. It might be in the leg at the other end. It might be right over the other side.'

'At least we can try.'

'I agree,' the PM said. 'But what happens if we don't get off in time?'

'Then both of you leave me,' said Masters.

The PM looked at Barker, who shrugged and

turned away. He stared at the bolted steel door and then turned back again.

'If you don't get off, they're going to find you,' said Barker.

'Not before I get their bomb.'

'Then they'll kill you. They'll definitely do that. They won't like what you've done.'

'It's the only way.'

'No. Let's call their bluff.'

'No, we can't call their bluff. You know they're not bluffing.'

Barker looked at the floor, his shoulders slumped in fatigue and dread, but he soon regained control of himself and gave Masters a painful grin. 'OK,' he said. 'Let's go.'

'Can you work the radio?' Masters asked.

'Of course,' Barker replied.

'Good. Get in touch with Bravo 1 while I remove the trapdoor. Tell them we want a helicopter. Say we want it right now. Tell them to make sure that they fly by the chart route and that they stay at low altitude all the way. We'll be in a small boat. We'll be five miles north-east of the rig. Tell them to keep their eyes peeled because we'll want picking up. They should have the harness ready. They should search around in that area. When we see them, we'll send up a flare and they can come down and get us.'

'I've got it,' Barker said. 'Now what about this

radio? I think we should knock this out as well, once we've used it ourselves.'

'No,' Masters said. 'They can't detect us with a radio. And we'll still need communication with the terrorists when we get back to Bravo 1.'

'*If* we get back,' Barker said.

'Yes, *if* we get back.'

They went to work. Barker turned on the radio. Masters crawled under the operator's console and reached out to the steel plate. It had a small handle set flush with the steel plate. Masters raised the handle and the plate came out with a harsh, grating sound. He laid it aside. The PM glanced at the hole it left. There was no sound of movement, so clearly the noise hadn't been heard out there.

Meanwhile Barker was on the radio, getting in touch with Bravo 1. He had the volume turned down low and the other two heard him whispering into the microphone. Masters crawled from under the console, stood up, wiped his hands on his overalls and then grinned at the PM. The latter was watching Barker, listening to what he was saying; Barker was talking in nautical terms and arranging the pick-up. After finishing, he turned off the radio and told the other two: 'It's all set.'

Masters went to the table, picked up a box of matches, and put them in the pocket of his overalls.

'Right,' he said to the Prime Minister. 'Please

listen carefully, sir. Barker here knows the rig well, so he's going to guide you. You'll go down through that hole. There's a steel ladder below it and it goes down twenty feet. I want you to go down carefully and wait at the bottom. You should be hidden by the crates. Barker's going first, so he'll already be down there and he'll guide you the rest of the way. It's pretty simple – but dangerous. There's a door right by the ladder. It leads to the outside of the rig just beneath the main deck. That ladder drops to a catwalk that's on top of the pontoon leg, running down two hundred feet to the loading barge. Don't look down or you'll get dizzy. And don't let go for a second. You'll be hanging on the outside of the pontoon leg and the wind there is rough. The deck stretches out above you. That means the terrorists won't see you. They might see you when you jump on the loading barge, but I think it's too dark. You'll both wait for me there. Give me forty minutes from now. If, by that time, I don't show up, just get in a small boat. Barker knows how to use them. He'll take you out to where the helicopter should be hovering, and they'll pick you both up.'

'Fine,' the PM said unconvincingly, taking a deep breath and letting it out slowly. 'So what about you?'

'If I don't show up, I've been caught. You'll find out soon enough. The terrorists are bound to ring Bravo 1 and give you the good news.'

'And what do we do then?'

'You can go back to square one. You can either give in to their demands or let them blow up the rig.'

The PM stared at him and was aware only or his grey, driven eyes. He looked at Barker, who just nodded, and they went to the console. Barker crawled under first, then slithered down through the opening. He kicked at air until his feet found the ladder, then his head and hands disappeared. The PM smiled bleakly, then knelt on the floor. He crawled under the console, put his legs through the hole, found the ladder and started lowering himself down. He glanced back up at Masters, who was waiting to follow him. The PM, knowing he might not see him again, grinned at him and waved. 'Good luck,' he said, then dropped down through the hole.

Masters waited for a moment, gazing around the radio shack, listening carefully at the door, then went to the console and disappeared into the darkness below.

11

Standing on the ladder just beneath the radio shack, Masters pulled the steel cover back over the hole. It dropped back into place and he checked that it was secure. There was a good chance that when McGee entered the hut he wouldn't notice the trapdoor. Then Masters looked around and saw the ceiling of the drilling floor. He was twenty feet above the floor, just above the packing crates, and he looked beyond them at the large, cluttered workshop, the pipes and chains of the moonpool. It was very quiet out there, with no work going on. He saw some terrorists wandering lazily to and fro, holding MP5 sub-machine-guns in their hands, though not at the ready. They seemed very far away and their conversation echoed dully. The lights blazed and the machinery cast great shadows that swallowed whole areas.

As Masters climbed down the ladder, the drilling floor disappeared. The packing crates were piled high above his head when he stood on the lower floor. The floor rose and fell, swaying gently from side to side. The Prime Minister was about five feet away, standing close to the wall. There was a steel door beside him, and the handle squeaked when Barker turned it. Barker winced and glanced over his shoulder and nodded at Masters, who nodded back, gesturing for him to continue. Barker carefully pulled the large handle down until it locked into place. The sound of the lock echoed, seeming louder than it was. Masters turned away to peer through the packing crates at the vast, silent drilling floor.

None of the terrorists had heard the sound. They continued wandering back and forth, moving in and out of the shadows, talking lazily, bored by their vigil.

Masters turned back to Barker as he was pulling the door open. He stepped outside and waved to the PM, who hesitated, then followed him. Masters waited till they had gone, then checked the drilling floor again. There was no sign that anyone had noticed their activity, so he walked through the door.

He was slapped by an icy wind, which beat and moaned around him. He was on the catwalk of a circular deck that was thirty feet wide. It was the top of a pontoon leg, and the main deck loomed above it. The leg plunged two hundred feet to the sea, where reflected lights slid over the waves. The catwalk was dark and the surrounding night was black with clouds. The wind moaned and rushed in from the sea and he heard the waves hammering, smashing against the pontoon leg. Masters turned back and closed the door behind him, making sure it was locked.

'I can't do it,' the PM said, looking down through the catwalk. He was staring at the ladder that was fixed to the huge leg and dropped vertically to the sea way below. It was exposed to the beating wind. He would have to climb down that two hundred feet and he just couldn't face it.

'Don't look,' Masters whispered. 'Just forget it. Just get on and climb down.'

The wind howled around the catwalk, beating and tugging at the Prime Minister. Gripping the railing and shivering with cold, he was looking down fearfully at Barker, now already on the ladder, hanging in an all-enveloping darkness with nothing below him.

'Go down!' Masters snapped.

He grabbed the PM's shoulder, shook him roughly and pushed him down. The PM trembled visibly, licked his lips and then murmured: 'Oh, God!' He turned his back to the sea, gripped the railing even tighter, put his right foot on the step just above Barker's head and followed him as he started his descent.

Masters watched them go down, which they did very slowly, hanging in a black, howling void without shape or dimension. The sea wasn't really visible: the darkness just fell down and deepened. The silvery-grey head of the PM was bobbing in the middle of nothing. The wind howled around the ladder, and Masters heard it rattling. He looked down and saw the grey head disappearing, watched it melting in darkness.

Masters dropped to one knee, kneeling in front of another trapdoor. He grabbed the handle, pulled up the steel plate and looked into a black, seemingly bottomless pit. There were rumblings in that darkness and the noise reverberated. The pit, which was the interior of the huge pontoon leg, was circular and thirty feet in diameter.

Masters lowered himself in and the icy air clamped around him. His right foot kicked the side and found the ladder, then his other foot followed. He climbed down a few rungs, then reached out for a switch. When he turned the lights on, he looked down and saw the dizzying depths.

The pontoons were filled with water which rose halfway up the leg, splashing up and down as the tapering leg swayed from side to side. The circular wall was webbed with ladders that ran down into the water, tapering off into single lines before they finally disappeared.

Feeling dizzy and claustrophobic, Masters almost stopped breathing. The water outside the leg made a hollow, drumming sound; the water inside, in that shadowed pit below, splashed and sent up its echoes. Masters looked to his right and saw a black, three-foot hole. It was the entrance to one of the support legs and it echoed as well.

He looked into the support leg and saw the glint of steel through darkness. The knowledge that he would have to crawl down there made him feel queasy. Reaching up above his head, he pulled down the steel cover. It clanged shut and the noise reverberated up and down the main leg.

Masters started his descent, moving slowly and carefully, hearing the echo of his footsteps on the ladder, watching the wall rise above him. He didn't look up – only left and right. He closed his eye when he passed the dimmed lamps, and moved through shadow and light. The leg was swaying from side to side. The curved walls creaked and shuddered. The waves outside the leg pounded dully; the water inside was splashing.

Masters kept going down, passing girders that formed shelves around the wall, red with rust, strewn with debris. The divers often came down here, leaving plastic cups and bits of wire. Masters felt a brief annoyance when he saw this, but he kept going down.

He kept looking from left to right. He was convinced the bomb was here. He was sweating fifty feet above the water when he finally saw it.

The bomb was resting on a narrow girder that

circled around the wall, about two feet away from Masters's head. As Masters had expected, it was the size of a tea chest, had a slotted iron frame, and was attached to the base of the girder with two cast-iron clamps.

There was no dynamite.

Masters cursed his own ignorance. Of course there wouldn't be dynamite. The plutonium metal core would be surrounded by TNT and packed tight inside the sealed explosive shell. Masters swore again, his voice echoing and returning. He gripped the ladder as it swayed from side to side, as the shadows fell over him. Still, he had found the bomb. Now at least he could dismantle it. Reaching out, he nearly fell off the ladder, so he grabbed it again.

Cursing, he just hung there. The ladder swayed with the pontoon leg. The shadows darted up and down the rusted steel, changed their shapes, crept around him. He remained on the ladder, hearing the water far below, recalling that the men who worked here were normally tied on with safety straps. But he had no safety straps; he had nothing to hold him on. He would have to climb up on that girder and do it from there.

Masters briefly closed his eyes and pressed his forehead against the ladder. As he felt it swaying gently from side to side, he heard the water below. He didn't want to look down. That vertical tunnel was terrifying. It plunged down to the water, which now looked much darker than the sea. Masters opened his eyes and felt the sweat on his brow. He heard the rumbling of the sea all around him as he moved up the ladder.

He climbed on to the girder, which was eighteen inches wide. On his knees, he pressed himself against the wall and tried not to look down. The glint of water caught his gaze. His eyes were drawn against their will. He looked down past the bomb, down that spiralling fifty feet, and saw the round pool of water far below, very black, deadly cold. Masters knew how cold it was and that he couldn't survive in it. If he fell, and if he couldn't find a ladder, he would freeze to death in five minutes.

He fixed his eyes on the bomb.

Disarming it was easy. He was surprised at his own skill. It was a skill that he had picked up in the Royal Marine Commando Munitions School, though not during work on live plutonium bombs. Still, he managed to do it, as the basic principles were the same, requiring only his pocket screwdriver and past experience. He pulled the connecting wires loose, unscrewed the explosive lenses, then dropped the separate pieces into the water fifty feet below. When he had finished, he loosened the clamps and tried to push the bomb off the ledge. But he couldn't budge it an inch – it was too heavy to move. Smacking it with the palm of his hand in frustration, he decided to leave it.

According to his watch he had nineteen minutes left. He felt a cold, sneaking panic that made him crawl back up the ladder. Reaching out with one hand, he grabbed the ladder and swung back down, kicked out with his feet and found the rungs and then hauled himself up.

He felt better as he ascended and saw the roof of the leg above him. It was swaying from side to side and creaking loudly, but this didn't concern him now. He kept going up, feeling a warming exultation; it was born of his need to escape from this chill prison. This mood carried him upward, rekindling his fire. Then he reached the narrow entrance to the support leg and his panic returned.

The support leg was three feet wide and merely part of an immense steel web. The support legs criss-crossed beneath the decks and ran down to the pontoons. Masters had to go down there, but he really didn't want to do it. Instead, he wanted to climb out of this leg and breathe the fresh air. Yet he had to cross the rig in order to reach the drilling room, located in a module on the drilling floor, just beyond the moonpool. As he couldn't get to the drilling floor, he simply had to go under it. He could do so by going down this support leg until it joined with another. That was sixty feet down. From there he could climb the other leg. That second leg, also sixty feet long, would bring him out on to the lower deck, not too far from the drilling room.

Masters clung to the ladder, looking down the support leg. It was narrow and its ladder fell steeply and disappeared into darkness.

Not having a choice, he started down the support leg, his footsteps echoing as he stepped on each rung, his own breathing amplified. It seemed to take a long time. In fact, it took no time at all. Conscious only of the ringing of his steel-tipped boots, he soon started climbing. The climbing was worse. He kept straining to see the top. Looking up, he heard increasing noise, a dull cacophony of movement. It was the rattling of chains and the clanging of pipes: the general background noise of a rig that was no longer working. The noises made Masters dwell on the world outside; they made him think of the terrorists on the deck and of the time he had left. Yet he finally reached the top. There was a catwalk and a door. Opening the door carefully, he looked out and was blinded by light.

He was on the storage deck and its wall lamps were blazing, illuminating the crates and throwing great shadows across the floor. Masters glanced left and right, but saw no sign of movement, so he stepped out and walked across the steel deck until he came to another door. He opened this and walked through, then climbed up another ladder. There was a low, narrow corridor at the top, leading out to the drilling floor. Masters didn't go out there, but instead turned left near the exit. He went straight up another steel ladder and walked into a module, located just above the drilling deck. Looking down, he could see the terrorists, wandering back and forth past the moonpool, talking and laughing. The deck was cluttered with equipment, the bright light cast stark shadows, and the men were all carrying their weapons in a careless manner.

Masters entered another corridor, which was bright and low-ceilinged. A man stepped out of a doorway just ahead and nodded curtly and brushed past. Masters walked to that doorway, heard the sound of a TV monitor, looked in and saw a man in a chair, looking up at the screen. The cameras were searching the seabed, scanning over the anchor chains. The bottom was four hundred feet down and the whole view was murky. The man had his back to Masters, his feet up on the desk, and seemed bored as he coughed into his clenched fist and gazed at the monitor. His weapon was leaning against the desk – an MAS Combat Rifle. There was a pile of hand-grenades on the table close by the terrorist's booted feet. Masters glanced at the floor and saw some magazines for the gun. The man coughed again into his clenched fist, clearing phlegm from his throat.

Masters walked up behind him, moving swiftly

and silently, to bring the edge of his calloused palm down on the terrorist's neck, at the side of the throat. The man didn't cry out; he simply grunted and slumped forward. Masters confirmed that he was dead, then closed the door. The monitor above the dead man was still showing the murky seabed.

Looking out through the window at the floor twelve feet below, Masters saw the terrorists gathered around the moonpool, smoking and drinking beer, leaving their weapons scattered carelessly on the deck nearby. They appeared to be having a break and Masters didn't like that.

He turned off the monitor, then switched off its power supply. Opening a box in the wall, he found the fuses amid a tangle of wiring. He pulled out some of the wires, quickly tied them together, then pushed them back against the wall and closed the box. The monitor was dead. The terrorists, finding it that way, would turn on its power supply. That's all Masters needed: the crossed wires would do the rest. The whole system would ignite and burn out beyond hope of repair.

A corpse would cause panic, so Masters had to move the dead man. He wanted the terrorists to find the room empty and think the man had just bunked off. But first he checked the grenades, which were not hand-grenades, but ones for use with the launcher that was attached to the barrel of the combat rifle. It was just what he needed.

Masters put on the belt to which the grenades were clipped. Opening the door, he glanced out and saw no sign of movement. Satisfied, he went back to the dead man, pulled him from the chair, and dragged him laboriously out into the corridor, where he hauled him along to the next door, a small storage room. After hurriedly bundling the corpse into that room, Masters returned to the drilling room, where he picked up the combat rifle and then casually walked out.

According to his watch, he had just under ten minutes left. He climbed down the steel ladder and turned left and walked on to the drilling deck.

The terrorists he had seen were still lounging around the moonpool, but others were wandering to and fro, in and out of the shadows. Masters simply started walking. It was a trick he had learnt somewhere. He knew that a total lack of self-consciousness could make people ignore you. He advanced across the drilling floor. A few passing men nodded. They glanced at him and looked away, as if they hadn't really seen him. He kept walking across the deck, passing through shadow and light, then climbed up steel steps and walked out of the drilling hut, emerging into the cold air of the main deck.

The derricks towered above him. The lights

tapered up into nothing. Floodlights beamed down on the deck, illuminating the terrorists. They were wandering back and forth, carrying AK47 assault rifles and MP5 sub-machine-guns, walking under the massive cranes, past the stacked pipes, with the darkness beyond them. Ignoring them, Masters made his way to the end of the deck until he was parallel to the radio shack. The same two guards were still standing outside the door, looking bored and lethargic.

Masters checked the time: he had five minutes left. He started walking along the edge of the deck, towards the radio shack. The sea murmured far below and the wind howled across him, but he made it to the hut and then slipped in behind it. It was very dark in there. He glimpsed the corner of the rig. Glancing down, he saw the huge pontoon leg, disappearing in darkness. He thought of Barker and the Prime Minister, silently praying that they had made it. They should both be down there in the barge, checking the time. Masters looked up again, beyond the roof of the radio shack; he saw the radar antennae thrusting skyward, halfway down the deck.

Breathing deeply, he put his arm through the sling of the rifle, then carefully climbed the ladder right in front of him. He reached the roof of the radio shack, slithered across it on his belly, only stopping when he reached the far edge and could see the whole deck. There he made himself comfortable, but remained on his belly. He pulled the rifle off his shoulder, checked the magazine, ensured that the grenade-launcher was working, then took the safety-catch off. The guards below made no sound. Masters looked along the deck, where the radar antennae were being bent by the wind.

He had one minute left. Still on his belly, he adopted the firing position and took aim with the combat rifle. The two guards were still below him, but the others were far away. Masters aimed at the guard to his left and then fired the first shot.

There was a crack; it was not very loud at all. The guard jerked violently, staggered in a circle, then went down. The other guard dropped to his knees, turning around, raising his weapon, looking shadowy and unreal in the gloom as Masters aimed for his chest. The rifle cracked again in his ear. The guard's arms flew out sideways. He spun away but had not yet hit the deck when Masters rolled from the edge.

He heard shouts and running feet, then the roar of many guns. Knowing they were confused, he reset his rifle and fixed a grenade to the barrel-mounted launcher. The running feet were approaching. A machine-gun stuttered. Still on his belly, he twisted to the side and aimed his rifle at the radar antennae. He didn't have much time. The shouting and shooting were spreading. He took aim at the base of the antennae and fired the grenade. It seemed to take a long time. Shadowy figures advanced towards him. Guns flashed and then he saw the flaring, silvery-white explosion, followed instantly by a roaring and the screeching of scorched, buckling metal.

He didn't wait to check the damage, but instead attached a second grenade, took aim and squeezed the trigger. He felt the recoil as the butt punched his shoulder. The second blast seemed even louder, with metal shrieking over the explosion as the antennae burned, buckled and twisted in searing white heat.

Masters put another grenade in the launcher and fired it at the terrorists. It exploded in the darkness, flared up and faded away. The antennae swayed to and fro, then caved in before the wind and crashed down over the deck and the running men. Steel exploded in all directions, a shower of sparks shot skyward, as Masters slithered back across the flat roof and climbed down to the deck.

He was behind the radio shack, on the corner of the rig, and looking down he thought he saw the sea below, a black mat in the void. The wind was pushing him against the wall as he fought his way to the catwalk. He saw a steel ladder that ran down past the decks to the top of the pontoon leg. Starting the climb down, he heard gunshots and shouting. He also heard the door of the radio shack banging against the wall, followed by McGee's voice bawling angrily.

Masters had no time to deal with McGee, so he kept climbing down. The wind howled and tried to sweep him from the rungs, but he didn't dare stop.

He finally reached the pontoon leg, where the wind howled dementedly, but he found the hole in the catwalk, put his feet on the ladder, and started to descend once more. It took a very long time. He passed under the lower deck. Looking through the silvery web of the supporting legs, he saw the darkness beyond. The wind here was fierce, howling under the rig. He glanced up and saw searchlights beaming down, raking the sea below.

Masters clambered down as fast as possible, hearing the firing of guns above his head, very high up and muffled. Then he heard the clang of boots above. There was shouting and the ladder vibrated and he knew they were following him. He climbed down even faster, forgetting the wind and the dreadful height, hearing the smashing of the sea against the legs, a dull metallic cacophony. The men above were shouting. That made him move faster. He climbed down and heard the roaring of a motor launch and knew that Barker was leaving.

He started yelling crazily, letting Barker know who he was, as the rifle slung over his shoulder pummelled his ribs.

Masters jumped from the ladder and fell down through darkness. He landed on the barge and rolled over and crashed into some crates. Barker called out his name, not sure what was happening. Masters jumped up and stumbled across the deck, hitting boxes and cables.

Suddenly, he saw Barker, not too far away, silhouetted against the cloudy night, at the prow of the loading barge. He lurched towards him, but he disappeared from view, then Masters reached the prow and saw the boat below him. Barker was at the wheel. The Prime Minister was waving at him. The sea was rough and the engine was roaring as Masters jumped down, almost hitting the PM, before crashing into the cabin wall. Barker ceded his place at the wheel to the SBS man and the engine roared louder as the boat moved off.

They saw the rig high above them, and searchlights beaming down on the water, then heard the gunfire. Wood splintered all around them. Barker screamed and threw his hands up. Masters saw his eyes, in them an awful incomprehension, before he jerked back and appeared to somersault and went over the side.

There was no point in stopping.

12

The small boat's motor roared against the wind. The sea was rough and it sloshed across the deck and drenched Masters as he struggled with the wheel. He heard the louder roar of the guns as the terrorists fired from the loading barge. They were shouting and then another engine growled into life, which meant they were following him. He glanced back over his shoulder and saw the Prime Minister at the stern, fully exposed to the gunfire, gazing into the water.

'Get down!' Masters shouted. 'Get your head down! They're trying to kill you!'

An automatic rifle cracked and he heard the bullets whipping past him. Fragments of wood exploded off the prow of the boat and as Masters dropped low the wheel started spinning. Cursing, he glanced up and saw the rig soaring above him, its many lights blazing out of the darkness. Glancing back, he saw that the PM was crouching low, peering from the stern of the boat, trying to see the men following them.

'Keep down!' Masters bawled.

'What about Barker?' the PM shouted back. 'I can see him! He's floating out there in the water! I'm sure I can see him!'

The boat had gone into a spin with waves sloshing across the deck, then it rose and plunged down into the waves, almost submerged. Masters jumped up, reaching for the runaway wheel. The terrorists' guns barked and more splinters of wood flew about him as he yanked the wheel back. The boat started straightening out, heading away from the oil rig. He heard the terrorists' launch ploughing through the waves as more bullets whipped past him.

'What about Barker?' the PM shouted above the roar of the motor and the sea.

'It's too late!' Masters yelled back.

'We can't just leave him!'

'There's no choice! Keep your head down, sir!'

Masters gave the engine full throttle, and the launch nosed up and plunged back down through the spray and waves. The PM yelped with shock as he stumbled back to Masters; soaked to the skin, he was looking down at himself as if not quite believing it. 'It's freezing cold!' he shouted. Masters didn't respond. He was gripping the wheel and heading into the darkness, the rough sea and the cutting wind. As the boat rose and fell the PM held on to the side. From behind they heard the rumble of the other boat and the shouts of the terrorists.

'They're following us!' the PM shouted.

'I know that!'

'Is there anything I can do to help?'

'Just keep your head down!'

Sub-machine-guns snapped behind them and bullets whined past on both sides. The PM dropped low behind Masters and mumbled something inaudible. Glancing back over his shoulder, Masters was temporarily blinded by a searchlight that passed across the boat, wavered, then came back towards him. He glanced down. The PM was crouched low. Masters grabbed him by the shoulders and tugged him up and placed his hands on the wheel.

'Hold her steady!' Masters shouted. 'Don't let the wheel move! Don't let the boat change direction!'

The PM's eyes widened, staring at Masters as if stunned, but he grabbed the wheel and looked straight ahead at the dark, surging sea. Masters unslung his combat rifle, then he heard the snap of automatic fire from behind him and dropped to the deck. The sea growled and washed over him as he crawled to the stern. There he looked up just as the searchlight found him, filling the launch with a dazzling light. The PM was exposed, so there really wasn't time to spare. Masters set the weapon on automatic fire, then aimed directly at the source of the blinding light. He could hardly keep his eyes open and the boat was pitching wildly, but he fired a short burst, a second, then a third, and was blessed with the distant sound of smashing glass as the darkness rushed back in.

He had knocked out their searchlight, but this respite was all too brief. He knew that the terrorist boat would have flares and emergency lights. Still growling behind him, banging noisily through the waves, it was starting to catch up. Masters hurried back along the boat to find the PM still holding the steering wheel. When the PM saw Masters, he gave a shy smile, as if embarrassed to be there.

'I'm no good at this,' he said.

'You're doing fine, sir.'

'I don't think I'll ever forget this experience.'

'I'm sure you won't, sir.' Masters took over the steering wheel once more. 'Can you fire a rifle?' he asked.

'No,' the PM replied. 'I'm no good at that either.'

The wind howled about them, the boat bucked and plunged back down, and the water sloshed across the deck to their rear and poured back out again. Masters held a steady course and knew just where he was going. Glancing briefly over his shoulder, he saw the lights of the distant rig, soaring up to the black sky, a diamond web illuminating the darkness. The other boat was closing the gap all the time, growing larger, a black shape on the light-flecked waves. Masters heard the men shouting and saw lamps flickering on, then another powerful light beamed down on the water and started inching towards him. Suddenly, the boat was looming large to the stern, cutting around Masters to run parallel to him.

'They've caught up!' the PM called out.

'Not for long,' Masters rasped, reaching down to grab a rope from the deck and lash the steering wheel to its support. 'Get into the cabin!' he shouted, but the PM just stared at him. The guns roared and Masters grabbed the PM and threw him down to the deck. 'In the cabin!' he bellowed. 'Get in the cabin! Move!' The terrorists' guns roared and again wood fragmented all around Masters, so he grabbed the PM by the shoulders and threw him bodily towards the steps. The PM crawled forward and made his way down the steps. Masters glanced at the wheel and saw that the rope was holding it steady. Reassured, he crawled forward as a stream of bullets stitched the whole boat, causing large chunks of wood as well as splinters to fly through the air.

He went to the starboard side, huddled up there and waited, listening to the rumbling of the other boat as it attempted to come close enough for the terrorists to board him. The terrorists were excited, shouting a lot as they fired their weapons. Masters heard their boat crashing through the waves, coming closer each second. Still, he didn't move. The sea hissed as it poured over him. The guns roared and bullets riddled the deck near the stern and made streams of water shoot upwards either side of the boat. Masters cursed: they were punctured below the water-line. He could tell by the noise that the other boat was coming in broadside. It was practically on top of him and would ram him any moment now.

Masters unclipped an American M26 hand-grenade, pulled the pin out, then jumped up and threw it. The other boat filled his whole vision. He saw the crazed eyes of his pursuers. They seemed startled as the grenade sailed through the air and he dropped low again. The grenade exploded with a deafening, staccato roar. He heard shrieks and the sound of tumbling bodies as he stood up again. He fired his combat rifle, still set on automatic, without looking. White flames were daggering up from the other boat, silhouetting the spinning, staggering men. Masters kept firing in short bursts, spraying the deck from prow to stern. Men screamed and tumbled over the sides or threw themselves to the deck.

The boat was pulling away from him, obviously out of control, with yellow flames licking over the wheel-house, turning blue, edged with black smoke. The grenade had ignited their spare petrol and the flames hissed and crackled.

A silhouette was jerking frantically by the smoking wheel-house – on fire, screaming dreadfully. Masters fired a burst at him and the burning man fell. A light winked and Masters dropped to the deck and heard the roar of the gun. He crawled back to the wheel-house, reached up and untied the rope. Opening the engine, he let the boat rush forward, then turned it to starboard.

The Prime Minister reappeared, looking up from the wheel-house steps. Masters told him to stay there, but the PM ignored him and clambered up the steps to crouch beside him. They both looked back and saw that the burning boat was falling well behind them, the flames clawing at the darkness and casting shadows on the sea's glowing surface. Human screams rose up from the water near where the blazing launch was drifting, out of control. Their own boat was now circling around it, cutting across to its starboard side.

The PM glanced at Masters, wondering what he was doing. Looking back, he saw the flames of the burning boat, which was turning and bobbing, moving across on their right, drifting very close to them. An inflatable dinghy had been thrown over the side, into the sea, and some terrorists clambered down on a rope ladder and fell into the dinghy. More screaming came from the deck – someone burning to death. The terrorists in the dinghy started rowing as the yellow flames licked out over them.

'Take the wheel,' Masters said.

The Prime Minister took the wheel, hardly thinking, just watching. Masters had turned the engine off and the little launch was just drifting. The PM held it steady as Masters picked up his rifle and aimed it at the terrorists in the dinghy. 'No, Masters!' the PM shouted. 'For God's sake, you can't . . .' But Masters was ignoring him and taking careful, deliberate aim. The PM released the wheel and rushed at Masters and tried pushing the gun up. Masters cursed, grabbed his shoulder and threw him aside. 'Damn it, let me go!' he said harshly. 'I won't let them go back!'

The PM stood where he was, shocked by Masters's venom. He glanced across the choppy, freezing sea at the men in the dinghy. Then Masters fired. It was a short, decisive burst. Someone screamed and a man threw up his hands and splashed over the side. Masters lowered the weapon. Air hissed out of the dinghy. The men shouted and waved their arms wildly as the dinghy collapsed. The PM closed his eyes, listening to their frightened screaming. Opening his eyes, he saw them splashing in the water and swimming frantically towards him. Masters went back to the wheel-house and turned the motor on. The launch growled and the water boiled around it as it moved away from the swimming men. Their cries for help were loud and clear. The PM was in shock. Masters steered a wide arc around the burning vessel and headed into the darkness.

Looking back, the PM saw the other launch sinking slowly. He heard the pleas of the men in the water, first receding, then fading out completely as the darkness took over.

'They'll freeze to death,' the PM said.

'That's right,' Masters said. 'But at least they won't go back to that bastard McGee and help him tomorrow.'

He headed out to sea, keeping the launch on an even course, while the PM lowered himself to the deck, stunned and exhausted. The darkness was all around him, having swallowed the terrorists' boat; the lights of the rig had long since vanished and the moon hid behind the clouds. Drenched and extremely cold, shocked by what he had witnessed, the PM gave in to a fear that he could scarcely control.

Masters's ruthlessness had startled him. He understood it, but it had unnerved him. Knowing that Masters was a sergeant in the legendary SBS, he also knew just how well he had been trained and how courageous he had to be. Masters lived in another world, one in which violent death was the norm; he had been trained to use his wits and not give in to doubt; and to kill without hesitation when he deemed it necessary. Now, with all the skills at his command, he would ensure, even at the cost of the lives of the terrorists, that he, his Prime Minister, would be returned safe and sound.

In Masters's view, the PM knew, the terrorists burnt alive, drowned or frozen to death in the sea behind him had merely received their just rewards. This knowledge was what frightened the PM, but he could not avoid the truth. The others had died that he might live and he and Masters both knew it.

They soon heard the rescue helicopter. It was flying from east to west just ahead at a very low altitude. Masters immediately stopped the boat, then went back to the stern. The deck had been shot full of holes and the water was pouring in.

'We were lucky,' he said. 'Another ten minutes and we'd have sunk. We'd have frozen to death just like that lot.'

He threw the anchor overboard and returned to the wheel-house, where he rummaged about on the floor, then stood up with a flare gun, which he aimed at the sky. There was a short, dull explosion. The flare burst in the sky high above, streaking the darkness with green and purple light. Masters fired a second signal and the coloured streaks formed an umbrella, racing outward, then curving back down to fade above the dark sea.

The Dragonfly's pilot saw the flares and descended to approach. Soon the helicopter was hovering just above the boat, its props causing a whirlwind.

A searchlight cut through the darkness as the helicopter hovered thirty feet above them, swaying dangerously in the wind, its engine making a deafening noise. The spinning props whipped the air and made the sea swirl and roar, the waves rushing across the deck of the launch to drench the PM and Masters. They held on to the sides, blinking against the powerful light. Falling out of the Dragonfly, the abseil harness blew out wildly on the fierce wind. The PM looked up and saw the wildly swinging harness, then looked higher at the bottom of the helicopter and felt his head spinning. Masters was shouting and waving at him, trying to give him instructions. The PM glanced down and saw the water creeping over his ankles.

'. . . boat's going down!' Masters was shouting. 'We've no time to lose!'

When the PM reached out for the harness, it flew away from his grasp. The helicopter continued roaring above him, the waves rushed in to drench him. Masters reached for the harness and caught it, then waved at the PM, who stepped forward, gripping the side of the boat. The boat was rocking in the violent, surging water, sinking down at the stern. Masters indicated the harness, holding it up to the PM. He saw two loops for his arms, and an encircling belt, so he held his arms out. The boat rocked and he nearly fell. Masters was speaking, still trying to give instructions, but the

PM couldn't hear a word. Masters attached the harness to him, tightening the belt around him, as the wind continued howling about them.

The SBS sergeant stepped back and waved at the helicopter. The PM felt the pounding of his heart, an absurd, childish dread. The cable above him went taut and he sucked his breath in. He was picked up and flew out on the wind and then was swinging in mid-air.

The PM gripped the straps, gasped for breath and closed his eyes. His stomach heaved and he suddenly felt hollow, so he opened his eyes again. He heard the roar of the helicopter, felt himself swinging freely, and glanced down to see the sea far below, its dark waves flattening out. He kept swinging back and forth as he was winched up on the cable. The roaring of the helicopter increased and the wind beat more fiercely.

The PM swung in space, seeing dark sky and the sea, feeling the wind and tasting the salt in the air before being jerked up and in. Strong hands grabbed his shoulders and dragged him in farther, until he saw the cluttered interior of the helicopter and a pair of wide, staring eyes. Seeing these, the PM realized who he was: that he *was* the Prime Minister. He said his thanks to the nervous eyes, smiling kindly as he did so. Grateful, the young, wide-eyed Royal Navy loadmaster unclipped the harness, took it off the

PM, then threw it back out again and watched it fall to the sea.

The PM looked down and saw the dark sea. The boat below seemed too small to be real and its stern was sinking under the water. Masters stood on the prow, which was pointing at the sky. He swayed to and fro as if about to fall, then reached up to the harness. The sea washed across the boat, engulfing most of it. The prow suddenly lurched up and fell back and Masters jumped into space, swinging away from the sinking boat as it disappeared beneath the waves. Masters dangled momentarily in the harness and then started ascending.

It seemed to take a long time. The wind howled through the Dragonfly. Masters floated far below in the darkness, moving up, coming closer. Then his head appeared through the floor. The loadmaster hauled him in. Masters turned around and looked back through the doorway at the black void below. There was no sign of the boat. The sea was merging with the darkness. Masters gasped and rolled on to his back and just lay there and smiled.

'Now we've got them,' he said.

13

'The situation is this,' Masters said to his CO, Lieutenant-Colonel Edwards, and Captain Pancroft. 'The terrorist bomb is now inoperative. We've knocked out their radar. That means we can get close to the rig without being detected. I suggest that we do so and that we do it this morning, while it's dark, before the dawn breaks.'

'Right,' Captain Pancroft said keenly. 'First light is always the best time. Catch the buggers napping.'

Masters grinned at Rudy Pancroft. He admired him greatly. Captain Pancroft had often been referred to as a legend in his own lifetime for his sterling work with the anti-smuggling patrols in Hong Kong, his surveillance activities in the 'bandit country' of Northern Ireland and, in particular, his heroic performances during the war in the Falklands, which had ended only a few months earlier. He was a good man to know.

'I agree,' Lieutenant-Colonel Edwards said. 'The sooner we clear this mess up the better. So let's be getting on with it.'

The two officers wore the full Royal Marines uniform, including the Commando green beret, plus parachuting wings and a badge denoting that they were Swimmer Canoeists. Both also had numerous military awards stitched to their tunics. Compared with them, the other men in the boardroom of Bravo 1 looked almost anaemic.

Masters was standing at one end of the table, wearing spotless overalls. The Prime Minister was sitting at his right hand, in a new, dark-grey suit with white shirt and silk tie. The rest of the men looked tired and pale from lack of sleep and anxiety. Turner played nervously with his beard; Sir Reginald McMillan kept drumming his fingertips on the table; and only Dalton, the American troubleshooter, had managed to retain his sardonic, hard-edged pragmatism.

Turner glanced at the two immaculate RM officers and said: 'I'm still worried. Who the hell backed the terrorists? You say they've got a man aboard this rig. Which one of us is it?'

'It doesn't matter,' Sir Reginald said. 'We can sort that out later. What matters at the moment is Charlie 2. We have to get that rig back.'

'I disagree,' Dalton said. 'I think Turner has a point. If McGee says their man's aboard this rig, then that man could be dangerous. McGee said he was one of us. He's right here in this boardroom. If, as McGee said, he has a radio, he could contact the terrorists. If he did, we couldn't take them by surprise; they'd just be sitting there waiting. I don't think the SBS can launch a successful assault if the terrorists know they're on the way.'

There were twelve men around the table and they stared at one another, all of them suddenly uncomfortable, self-conscious and edgy.

'One of us?' a Frenchman asked.

'That's right,' Masters replied. 'They definitely said that the man was in this boardroom, so it could be me . . . you . . . *anyone*. We've no way of knowing.'

There was another lengthy silence. The men fidgeted, coughed, or stared at the table. The Under-Secretary put his chin in his hands and looked extremely annoyed.

'Incredible!' he exclaimed. 'Becoming more so every minute. This whole situation defies belief and it's truly quite sickening. First the terrorists sink a rig, then they take over another. Now we find that one of our own senior executives has ordered the assassination of the Prime Minister. I find this whole thing appalling.'

Sir Reginald sighed. 'We've been through all this before. Let's stick to the issue at hand and sort this mess out.'

'It's *your* mess,' the Under-Secretary told him. 'And it's a disgusting mess. The lack of security throughout your organization is utterly scandalous.'

'I agree,' the PM said. 'I'm still appalled by the whole affair. If word of this ever gets out, the repercussions will be devastating to us all.'

'We'd be a laughing-stock,' the Under-Secretary said.

'Precisely,' the PM replied. 'Worse still: confidence in the viability of the North Sea would be lost internationally.'

'That's true enough,' Dalton said. 'My side would definitely pull out. I don't see any Americans staying in the North Sea if this mess is made known to them.'

They all slumped back into a silence that was filled with nervous coughing. More cigarettes and cigars were lit and their smoke turned the air blue.

'He has a radio,' Turner reminded them. 'Whoever he is, he has a radio. We better search every cabin in the rig and make sure we find it.'

'No,' Lieutenant-Colonel Edwards said. 'I don't think so. For one thing, he's possibly got rid of the radio already, to avoid being caught; for another, such a search is bound to arouse the suspicions of your crew. You want this kept as quiet as possible. If, as McGee says, the man is here in this boardroom, then let's just make sure he stays here. We'll attack the rig immediately. It'll all be over by first light. Until then, don't let anyone other than the SBS leave this boardroom. That should solve *that* particular problem.'

The CO glanced around the table. Most of the men seemed to be in agreement. The PM could not resist a slight smile when he gazed at Sir Reginald.

'And what then?' Dalton asked. 'We still have to find out who he is. If he can pull this stunt, he'll pull others and that isn't acceptable.'

'I think you should leave that problem until tomorrow,' Captain Pancroft said. 'Right now, the major concern is the recapture of the rig held by the terrorists.'

'I agree,' the PM said. 'We must get the terrorists off Charlie 2 and then hush this thing up. That's our prime concern.'

'But why attack?' Turner asked. 'I don't see the point. An assault like that requires a lot of men – and a lot will be killed. Why not just sit tight? The terrorists have lost their bomb. Why attack when we can just leave them there until their food runs out?

'It would take too long,' Masters said. 'Fresh supplies went out to Charlie 2 yesterday. That gives them four normal weeks, which they could stretch out much longer.'

'So what?' Turner responded. 'I say sweat them out.'

'No,' Dalton said. 'I back Masters in this. If we

let them sit on Charlie 2 for four weeks, they'll start using their radio. They'll talk to the press – to the whole damn media. Before we know it, the entire world will know about it. We have to prevent that.'

'The media will learn about it anyway,' Turner insisted. 'If we capture the terrorists, they'll talk. You can't keep a thing like this quiet. It's too big for secrecy.'

'I disagree,' the American said. 'Nothing's too big for silence. If the terrorists are captured, they'll be rushed straight into prison and allowed no access to the press. This is, after all, a matter of national security. On those grounds we can ensure that the trial takes place behind closed doors. The oil companies will then agree their own version of events, the terrorists will each be given twenty years to life, and by the time the dumb bastards are released this episode will be ancient history. And by then the North Sea will be drained dry of oil and we'll be drilling elsewhere.'

'That's important,' the Under-Secretary said. 'A total lock-up is vital. The only people who know about this affair are the terrorists and us, so we've got to make sure it remains that way.'

'The terrorists' backers know,' Turner reminded him.

'They won't talk,' Masters said. 'As McGee

kindly informed me: they can't ever discuss this affair without giving themselves away.'

'McGee really screwed them,' Dalton said.

'That's right,' Masters replied. 'He screwed them and now they have to sit tight and keep their mouths shut.'

'So,' the Prime Minister said. 'We attack them immediately. We launch a full-scale assault and get them off that rig, and then throw them in jail and forget about them.'

'Correct,' Dalton said. 'McGee's given us our story. We say it was an earthquake on the seabed. We put that out as our press release.'

'It's rather risky,' Sir Reginald said. 'We'll have to use a lot of men. I can't see how we're going to keep it quiet with so many men knowing.'

'*SBS* men,' Lieutenant-Colonel Edwards emphasized. 'My men always operate in strict secrecy and they *never* talk afterwards.'

'So,' Dalton said, 'we use the SBS to recapture the rig, then we put out our own press release and replace the whole crew with new men who don't know what's been happening. I think that solves the problem.'

He smiled and glanced around him, receiving nods of agreement from everyone except Masters, who was looking out through the nearest porthole at the dark Forties Field. He was recalling Barker standing up in the motor launch, his eyes widening with stunned disbelief as he went over the stern. Now Barker was dead and drifting somewhere out there; he was at the bottom of the sea with the other dead, rig workers and terrorists alike, and those bastards on Charlie 2 were responsible. Masters glanced at the Under-Secretary and saw his handsome, shocked face. He knew that the civil servant wasn't shocked by the body count; that his hatred of the oil companies had totally erased the dead from his thoughts. He was a political animal and this was all politics. In the end, it was *always* politics. Masters knew it and felt deep revulsion, but he had to live with it. He still had a job to do.

'All right,' the PM said gravely, after considerable thought. 'I authorize the assault.'

The wave of relief that passed around the table was jarred when the red telephone rang. Looking startled, Turner picked it up.

'I've got Charlie 2 on the line,' the operator informed him. 'They want to speak to the boardroom.'

Turner frowned. 'Anyone special?'

'No. It's their leader, McGee. He just wants the boardroom.'

Turner visibly trembled and focused on the floor. 'All right,' he said, sounding defeated as he switched to the open line. 'Tell him I'm here.'

McGee came on the phone, clearly angry, his voice hoarse. 'OK,' he said, 'you bastards fixed my bomb, but I'm not finished yet. Let me speak to Masters.'

There was a brief, tingling silence as Turner stood there with the receiver in his hand, not knowing what to do. Eventually, after nods of permission from the PM and Sir Reginald, he handed the phone to Masters.

'This is Masters speaking.'

'You're a smart bastard, Masters.'

'Thanks for the compliment,' Masters said. 'Now what do want?'

'I want your hide,' McGee said.

'You're not going to get it.'

'I just might. Sure, I'm not finished yet. I've something else up my sleeve.'

Masters glanced at the others around the table and saw the return of their fear. 'What's that, then?' he asked the terrorist leader.

'You think I'm dumb, Masters? You think you've fucking beat me? Well, don't think too soon.'

'What do you want?' Masters repeated.

'I want what I've always wanted. I want a million in cash and my four comrades out of the Maze.'

'You're too late,' Masters told him. 'You've nothing left to offer. You can't even bargain with your bomb. I took that away from you.'

'Ackaye, you did. But that doesn't mean I'm sitting here stranded. Not by a long chalk.'

'No?'

'No. Sure, if you weren't so fucking dumb you'd have guessed. I can still sink this rig.'

Masters glanced around the boardroom. The men sitting at the table leant forward, looking tense and confused.

'We came prepared,' McGee said. 'We've got plastic explosives. We can't blow up the whole of the Forties, but we can still sink this rig. I'll blow a pontoon leg off, Masters, and you know what that means. This whole fucking rig'll go down – and that isn't good news.'

Turner groaned audibly and covered his face with his hands. The other men looked at each other, some turning pale, but Dalton stood up, walked deliberately around the table, then stood beside Masters and studied him with eyes slightly narrowed.

'Plastic explosives?' Masters asked.

'Right,' McGee confirmed. 'Enough to blow a hole in one pontoon leg and sink the whole rig. And that, Masters, is what I'm gonna do if we don't agree right now.'

When Masters glanced at Dalton, the American shrugged and nodded, telling him to agree.

'All right,' Masters said. 'How do we do it?'

The PM stared disbelievingly at Dalton, who shrugged again, then raised his hands in the air in a gesture of resignation. Turner groaned, his head still in his hands, and Sir Reginald sighed.

'You've got till dawn,' McGee said. 'I don't need the Prime Minister. I've already stolen a million from our backers; I'll take the rest from you bastards. You'll deliver the cash by dawn. By helicopter. You'll personally fly the chopper, Masters, and then we'll have words. That leaves my four men in the Maze. I want them out by six a.m. tomorrow. I expect one of them to ring me as soon as they're all free and I also want the pardons announced in the evening papers in England.'

'And then?'

'We'll leave. Flying out by helicopter. We'll land on a private airstrip and then disappear and we'll keep our mouths shut as long as we're free and untouched. If you touch any of us, we'll talk; if you don't, we'll keep quiet.'

'Anything else?' Masters asked.

'No,' McGee said. 'You've got till dawn to fly here with the cash; if you don't, this rig sinks. And don't try a sneak attack. That wouldn't please me at all. At the first sign of an assault, we'll blow up the pontoon leg. That's all there is to it.'

There was a long silence. Masters sucked in his breath and then let it out again. His gaze came to rest on the portholes, on the darkness beyond. He coughed and took another deep breath and then let it out slowly.

'Agreed,' he said. 'Dawn.'

McGee rang off and Masters put the phone

down, then he scanned the many faces around the table. The PM leaned forward, scratching his chin, looking at the SBS man as if trying to take his measure. Masters offered a slight smile.

'Yes?' the PM asked.

'No,' Lieutenant-Colonel Edwards replied on Masters's behalf. 'We're going to take that rig back tonight. We'll start the whole thing right now.'

'We can't do that,' Sir Reginald insisted. 'We all heard what the man said. The minute he sniffs an attack, he'll blow a hole in that leg.'

'What does that mean?' the Under-Secretary asked.

'The rig will sink,' Turner explained.

'Can we afford to lose another one?' the PM asked. 'Can we sacrifice that much?'

'No,' Sir Reginald replied. 'I really don't think we can. Charlie 2 is the most important of all the rigs and we can't let it go.'

'Why the most important?' asked the Under-Secretary.

'It's a refinery,' Turner explained. 'It's a floating refinery, controlling the flow of all oil north of the Beryl Field.'

'I don't understand,' the Under-Secretary said. 'It's only one rig. Surely a single rig is disposable.'

'One more rig we can afford,' Turner said. 'But not Charlie 2.'

'Why?' the Under-Secretary persisted.

Turner stood up and went to the large map of the North Sea that was pinned to a blackboard. He placed his index finger on the Forties Field, moved it north to the Beryl Field, then moved it farther north until it passed Eagle 3 and came to rest well above the Frigg Field.

'More than half our oil – by which I mean the oil in the British sector – now flows from a single undersea pipeline linking the five major oilfields to Peterhead. As you can see, that single pipeline connects every major field north of the Forties Field. The oil from *all* the fields north of the Frigg Field flows down through Frigg, from there down to Beryl, through Beryl to here, and then on from here back to Peterhead. In this link-up, Charlie 2 acts as a refinery, controlling the speed of the oil flow. If McGee blows a hole in that leg, Charlie 2 will certainly sink – but to sink, it first has to topple over. That would almost certainly tear out the extractor pipes, which in turn would split the main pipes. We'd lose the oil then. The pipes would just break apart. The oil would pour into the sea and miles of pipe would be lost. We wouldn't be able to repair that damage – at least not for a long time – and in the meantime, all the oil north of here would be lost for good. That amounts to almost half our total output.'

'You mean *Britain's* output,' the Prime Minister emphasized.

'Yes, sir, Britain's output.'

'And what if we can't avoid this?' the PM asked. 'Just how bad would this be in general economic terms?'

'*Very* bad,' said the Under-Secretary, now on more familiar ground. 'Oil is our primary machine-driving fuel. We also need it for power stations and domestic fuel. It's also the raw material for all kinds of substances, such as plastics, and without it the petrochemical industry would die. As of this moment, Britain is dependent on oil for almost two-thirds of its fuel needs. To lose over half now, for the length of time envisaged by Mr Turner, would almost certainly be catastrophic.'

'All right, Mr Turner,' the PM said. 'Just how long *would* it take to repair the damage?'

'One to two years,' Turner replied, 'depending on weather conditions and always assuming that the damage *could* be repaired.'

'Also,' Sir Reginald cut in, 'since government taxation and British organized labour forced us to have the rigs made in France and Norway, rather than at home, those two countries, seeing our predicament – and being already annoyed by our ongoing concentration on US and Middle East markets – would doubtless get their own back by charging the earth for future rigs and by enticing foreign investors to deal only with them. In short, Prime Minister, it would be disastrous.'

The PM knotted his hands, cracked his knuckles, flexed his fingers, then glared at the Chairman.

'Laying the blame on this government,' he replied icily, 'is scarcely appropriate.'

'So,' Lieutenant-Colonel Edwards said, to avoid a lengthy debate. 'We attack them tonight.'

'If we attack them,' Sir Reginald responded stubbornly, 'they will sink Charlie 2.'

'No,' Masters said, 'they won't sink it. They'll just blow a hole in it.'

'And that won't sink it?' the PM asked.

'Not immediately,' Turner explained. 'It would take at least twenty minutes. It depends how big the hole is, but the SBS would have *some* time.'

'That's right,' Masters said. 'And the terrorists won't know we're coming. They won't know until we're actually on that rig, which gives us a head start.'

'The submersibles,' Captain Pancroft suggested.

'Exactly,' Lieutenant-Colonel Edwards said. 'We'll use our miniature submarines. They normally carry two men, but we can squeeze three men in each and still leave just enough room for the weapons. We'll leave from Peterhead. The boats will take us close to Charlie 2. About five miles from Charlie 2 we'll dive in the submersibles, travel to the rig, and surface right beneath the main deck. We can climb up the ladders. The terrorists won't be expecting us. A lot of the terrorists will be asleep, which is to our advantage. Another advantage is the weather. There's a storm due in three hours. If that makes our climbing difficult, it's also certain to make the terrorists more lethargic. So, we get on board. The first wave attacks the terrorists. While they're doing so, the second wave enters the damaged pontoon leg – we can assume the terrorists will have blown that hole in it by then – and blocks the hole up before the rig sinks. Once that's done, they return to the rig and help the other SBS troops mop up the terrorists.'

'This all sounds terribly efficient,' Sir Reginald said. 'But are you sure the terrorists won't see you approaching, even though you're submerged?'

'I don't think so,' Masters said, glancing at his CO and answering the question for him. 'I knocked out their radar and their undersea cameras, so they won't see us coming in. They might see us on the ladders, but that's a chance we'll have to take. Even if they *do* see us there, at least we can fight our way up. Obviously they'll blow that hole in the pontoon leg as soon as they see us, but we'll still have that twenty minutes left. If we manage to get down that leg in time, we should save the rig.'

'But the rig will still be damaged,' Sir Reginald insisted. 'It will be severely damaged by all the fighting.'

'That's true,' Masters replied. 'I'm afraid we'll have to accept that. But at least if we can keep it afloat, we'll be able to repair the damage that's been done. Besides, according to the story you're going to put out in your press release, that rig's supposed to have been damaged by an earthquake under the seabed – so I think it should look that way.'

'Good point,' Dalton said. 'As soon as the press release goes out, we'll see planes flying over. The media will want photos. They'll want to see a damaged rig. So *let* the terrorists knock the hell out of Charlie 2; it fits in with our story.'

The PM sat back to gaze at each of them in turn. Placing his hands flat on the table, he shook his head in amazement. 'I don't believe this,' he murmured.

'Let's do it,' Lieutenant-Colonel Edwards said. 'We have to hit that rig while it's dark and it's two o'clock now.'

'I agree,' Dalton said, pushing his chair back and rising to his feet. 'Let's get going. We've no time to waste.' Everyone stared at him in surprise. 'I'm going as well,' he explained. 'I want to have a talk with that McGee. I want to know who his backer is.'

'You can't go,' the Under-Secretary told him. 'The man who backed the terrorists is right here in this boardroom. We must all stay here until the SBS complete their attack. That's what was agreed.'

'With all due respect,' Turner replied, 'it hardly seems likely that Dalton would be that man since the survival of the rigs is in his own interests and those of his company.'

'I agree,' Lieutenant-Colonel Edwards said. 'If he wants to come, let him. Mr Dalton's not only widely experienced at counter-terrorism on behalf of the oil companies; he was also in the US Special Forces SEAL unit – the Amphibious Sea Air Land unit – which indeed is where he and I first met. So if he wants to come along, I have no objections.'

They all stared at the PM, who shrugged wearily and said: 'I agree.'

'Good,' Dalton said.

Silence reigned over the boardroom for what seemed like a long time, though it was, in fact, only a matter of seconds. There were rumblings outside, distant shouting and muffled banging; as usual, work was continuing throughout the night, conducted by roughnecks and roustabouts, oblivious to what was happening inside.

Masters glanced at his watch, then at the Prime Minister. He was held by the sharpness of the blue eyes in that flushed, knowing face.

'I'll stay here,' the PM said, addressing Lieutenant-Colonel Edwards. 'The rest of us will all stay here until it's over. I'll personally ensure that no one leaves this room until you give us a call.'

Edwards nodded, then smiled at Masters. Turner stood up and yawned and stretched himself as if no longer nervous. Masters glanced around the room.

It was bright and filled with smoke. The realization that it was two in the morning suddenly made him feel tired. He shook his head and rubbed his eyes, feeling slightly unreal. Opening his eyes, he saw Dalton grinning like a schoolboy as he walked to the door. Turner opened the door to let the American walk out. He was followed by the two SBS officers. Masters glanced this way and that, at the men around the table. Every one of them looked guilty as he walked from the room.

14

Walking with the others across the enormous platform, feeling the cold wind at his face, seeing the lights of the derricks tapering up to the dark sky, where the clouds formed a low, oppressive ceiling, Masters experienced a feeling of elation, a fresh surge of energy. He walked quickly and impatiently, between Edwards and Pancroft, just behind the enthusiastic Dalton, who appeared to be leading them. The American cut around the cranes and stacks of wooden crates, exposing them to an even stronger wind and the sound of the pounding sea. Reaching the end of the deck, he led the way up a steel ladder, then diagonally across a smaller deck to the cramped radio shack. The door was closed, but Dalton opened it and walked in, followed by the others. The operator looked up in surprise.

'Mr Dalton!' he exclaimed, fazed by the sudden appearance of the feared but respected figure.

'Take a break, kid,' Dalton said. 'Close the door after you.'

'Sorry?' said the operator.

'I want you to leave,' Dalton said.

'I'm not supposed to do that, Mr Dalton. You know I can't.'

Masters walked up and jerked his thumb towards the door. The operator, recognizing him as a top tool-pusher, stood up, looking very confused, and walked to the door. He left, but then stuck his head back in.

'Do I wait here?' he asked.

'That's right,' Masters said. 'Just wait there. When we want you, we'll call you.'

'Righto, chief!' the operator said chirpily, then stepped out and closed the door.

Masters sat at the radio, contacted onshore security, and told them to put Blackburn on as quickly as possible. The line was crackling with static. The storm was obviously brewing. After what seemed like a very long time, Blackburn came on the line.

'Masters?' Blackburn asked.

'Yes,' Masters said.

'What's up?' Blackburn asked. 'I was sleeping. This better be good.'

'It's an emergency, Andy. Can you connect us from here on a scrambled line to the SBS on hold at the old training centre at Achnacarry?'

'Sorry, Tone. I'd need higher authority for that. What the hell's going on?'

Dalton moved up behind Masters and leaned

down to the microphone. 'This is Paul Dalton,' he said. 'I'm your higher authority.'

'I'm sorry, sir, but I can't accept that. As far as I'm concerned, you could be anyone. Do you have your ID?'

'Good man,' Dalton said, then he recited the lengthy, confidential personal number by which he could be identified over the phone. There was a pause while Blackburn checked it in his pocketbook of ID numbers, then he said: 'Fine, sir. Go ahead.'

'I'm going to put the Commanding Officer of the SBS squadron at Achnacarry on the line. Lieutenant-Colonel Edwards. I want you to put him though to his second in command at Achnacarry. Understood?'

'Yes, sir, I've got it. Just bear with me a minute or so and I'll make the connection.'

'Scrambled.'

'Yes, sir.'

The radio emitted static that crackled loudly and faded out as Masters stood up and gave the chair to his CO. Lieutenant-Colonel Edwards sat patiently in front of the radio, listening to the rise and fall of the static until another voice came on the line: 'Lieutenant-Colonel Edwards?'

'Yes, this is Edwards. Please identify yourself.'

'Major Laurence Lockyard speaking.'

Edwards chuckled. 'That voice couldn't belong to anyone else, Major. You just sound a bit sleepy.'

'I'm in my pyjamas, boss, and was having a good sleep. What's up out there?'

'This is confidential, Laurence. I want a seal placed across it.'

'I didn't think you'd be using this line, boss, if that wasn't the case. So what's the situation?'

'Emergency. Action immediate. An oil rig has been seized by a large group of terrorists – sixty men – and we're going to launch an assault to take it back. It has to be before first light.'

'Read you loud and clear, boss.'

'The requirement is for five submersible-carrying boats to leave Peterhead as soon as you can get your men there. The lead boat, *Victory*, will carry four submersibles and the remaining four vessels will carry two each, making a total of twelve. The boats will sail directly to the Beryl Field. I want thirty-two battle-experienced SBS Marine Commandos to go with the twelve submersibles, with myself and three others, all here, making up a total compliment of thirty-six men. The men are to be equipped with full combat packs, including Sterling sub-machine-guns and Armalite rifles with M203 grenade-launchers. Six of the men will work as a maintenance team equipped with spare plates for the pontoon leg and emergency wet-welding equipment. Have you got that so far?'

'Yes, boss, I've got it.'

'Good.' Edwards coughed into his clenched fist,

clearing his throat, then continued in his clipped, precise manner: 'I want the boats to leave as soon as your men reach the secured dock at Peterhead. You will fly there by helicopter. The British United Oil security chief, Andy Blackburn, will be there to greet you and see you into the dock. Once the boats leave, I want them to sail with all due haste. The RV is five miles east of Charlie 2 on a grid reference being sent through on a burst transmission when Mr Blackburn informs us of your arrival at the Peterhead dock. Once at the RV, you will anchor and await my arrival. Launch the submersibles while you're waiting. We'll put three, repeat *three*, men plus weapons in each. You can tell them that they're going to make an assault against Charlie 2 and that I'll be giving them further instructions when I arrive. Place the maintenance team on hold. I'll be set down by chopper on *Victory* and will want to have a word with them, so don't let them get into their submersibles until I arrive. Is all that understood?'

'Understood, boss.'

'Can you give me an estimate for arrival time at the RV?'

There was a pause while Major Lockyard calculated the time required to gather the men together, get them into the helicopters, flying them from Achnacarry to Peterhead, transfer them to the boats, then carry them on the boats to the RV. Eventually, having completed his calculations, Lockyard said: 'About four hours.'

'That's too long,' Edwards told him.

'There's a limit to how fast those submersible-carriers can go. And, of course, there's the unpredictability of the weather. I can't promise a faster time than that.'

'It's too long,' Edwards insisted.

They all heard Lockyard sigh. 'How soon?'

'Three hours maximum,' Edwards said. 'I can't launch the assault later than 0600 hours, so that will give me four hours to co-ordinate everything.'

'I'll need at least an hour to get the men together,' Lockyard insisted, 'and get them into those choppers.'

'Cut that time down by half. You can make it in thirty minutes. Once you get to the docks, Blackburn will clear the way and ensure that you save another thirty minutes in getting to, and into, the boats. The journey from Peterhead to the Beryl Field should take no more than two hours. One and two makes three.'

This time they heard Major Lockyard chuckling. 'Right, boss, I'm convinced. We'll be at the RV in three hours. Anything else?'

'No.'

'Roger. Over.'

'Over and out.'

The radio went dead and a happier Lieutenant-Colonel Edwards sat back in the chair. 'So what about a helicopter?' he asked.

'I'll attend to it,' Masters said. He picked up a telephone and called the surgery of Bravo 1, then asked for Dr Seymour. When the doctor came on, Masters said: 'How's that American kid?'

'Schulman? He's OK, but he's sleeping.'

'Where?'

'In the surgery.'

'Drugged?'

'No, just sleepy. He had a couple of beers and fell asleep, so I just let him lie there.'

'Wake him up,' Masters said. 'Send him up to the bar. Tell him to be there in half an hour. I want to talk to him.'

'Will do,' Dr Seymour said.

Masters put the phone back in its cradle, then yawned and stretched himself.

'The good sergeant is tired,' Captain Pancroft said with a grin. 'We should put him to beddy-byes.'

'Instead of dragging him along on this mission,' the CO said sardonically. 'It's bound to be too much for him.'

'Do you think you can make it, Sergeant Masters?' Pancroft asked.

'I always finish what I start,' Masters informed him. 'It's the SBS way.'

'Good man,' Edwards said. 'Now let's get out of here.'

They all left the radio shack and found the operator standing outside. He was shivering and flapping his arms vigorously against the cold.

'Can I go in now?' he asked.

'You can go in,' Masters told him. 'But don't let anyone – and I mean *anyone* – make a call out. I don't care who it is.'

'I don't think I can argue with . . .'

'I'll authorize that,' Dalton said. 'Any arguments, use my name. And if anyone *does* comes to make a call, I want to know who they are.'

'Right, chief,' the operator said, then went into the hut and closed the door.

Dalton led the way across the deck and back down the ladder. The wind was growing stronger, moaning around the derricks, and the great platform was a patchwork of bright lights, white spaces and shadows. Walking across the main deck, they were surrounded by men still working, climbing up and down ladders, crossing catwalks, carrying crates and huge pipes. Dalton climbed another ladder, followed by Masters, then Edwards and Pancroft. They all entered the modules, made their way along narrow corridors, went down more steps and then found themselves in the canteen, also used as the bar. Some of the shift workers were eating, cutting into thick steaks with piles of chips. The three SBS men leant against the counter while Dalton ordered them coffees, just like one of the boys.

'When do we leave?' he asked, turning around to face Edwards.

'As soon as we can,' the CO replied.

'Just as soon as Schulman gets his chopper going,' Masters clarified. 'It won't do any harm to be early.'

'Do you think the boats will make it, Tone?'

'Yes, Paul, I do. That storm isn't due until 0600, so we should have a smooth trip. But the storm'll be rough. It won't make the climb easy. On the other hand, it'll put the terrorists off their guard. They won't expect us to arrive in such weather, so that could be a help.'

'Thirty-six men,' Pancroft said. 'Against sixty terrorists. I don't see that as good odds.'

'Shame on you,' Edwards admonished him. 'I'd have thought they were terrific odds for us. Not even two terrorists to each SBS man. Hardly worth another thought, Captain.'

'To hell with it,' Masters said, taking note of Pancroft's grin, but deciding to be serious all the same. 'We're just going to have to risk it. Besides, half the terrorists will be asleep. We can hit them really hard before they even get their eyes open. That should bring their numbers down, even the odds a little, and with the storm and the element of surprise they'll be pretty confused.'

'I hope so,' Pancroft said.

'What the hell!' Edwards exclaimed with a cheerful grin. 'It's all up for grabs now.'

They glanced repeatedly at their watches while drinking their coffee. The roustabouts and roughnecks at the tables were still eating, drinking, smoking and talking a lot. Masters was thinking how unreal it all was. Everything had taken place in twelve hours and these men had continued working right through it. They still didn't know about it and probably never would. They would read about an earthquake beneath the seabed that destroyed one oil rig, badly damaged another and killed many rig workers, and they would simply see it as part of the job, par for the course in the North Sea. Masters shook his head at the thought.

The four men had just finished their coffee and were returning their cups when Jack Schulman walked up to them.

'Hi,' said the helicopter pilot, grinning wryly at Masters, but looking curiously at Dalton and the two Royal Marine Commando officers with him.

'You look tired,' Masters told him.

'I *am* tired,' Schulman said. 'I'm fucking beat, so what the hell did you want me for?'

'We need you,' Masters said.

'At *this* hour?'

'At this hour.'

'Don't tell me another goddamn rig's sunk. I still haven't recovered from the last one.'

'No,' Masters said. 'It's nothing like that. We just want you to fly us out to Beryl. We have to fly there immediately.'

'Charlie 2?'

'Five miles east.'

'What the hell's there?'

'You'll find out soon enough,' Masters told him. 'Now go and get ready.'

Schulman, who still believed that Masters was a top tool-pusher, looked at the Royal Marine Commandos standing on either side of Dalton, but didn't ask what they were doing there. 'I don't believe this,' he said.

'You better believe it, Jack.'

'It's two-thirty in the morning, for Chrissakes. What the fuck's going on?'

'It's an emergency,' Masters said.

'Jesus Christ, not another.'

'The same one, in a sense,' Masters lied. 'Eagle 3 was the victim of an earthquake on the seabed. The bottom split open right beneath it, then that crack spread as far as the Beryl Field.'

'That's what sank Eagle 3?'

'That's what sank it,' Masters said firmly.

'And now the earthquake's gone as far as the Beryl Field?'

'Yep.'

'Here,' Dalton said. 'Have a coffee, kid. It might wake you up a bit.'

'Gee, thanks a lot, chief.' Schulman took the coffee, drank some, then wiped his lips with his hand. 'So what's happening out there in Beryl?'

'It's Charlie 2,' Masters told him. 'It's been badly damaged, so we're mounting a rescue operation.'

'From five miles east?' Schulman asked.

'That's right,' Masters said. 'We don't want to land the chopper because the rig might be sinking, so we're planning to move in slowly by boat.'

'I'm supposed to drop you on the boat?'

'In a nutshell,' Masters said. 'You drop us and then you fly back here and wait for our call.'

'If you get aboard I'll pick you up?'

'If we save the rig you'll pick us up.'

'So what if you don't save the rig?'

'Then we might go down with it.'

Schulman glanced at the men eating, as if yearning for steak and chips. 'OK,' he said, turning back to Masters, 'what time do we leave? I could do with a hearty meal.'

'We leave yesterday,' Masters said. 'We're a day late already. I want you to go straight up to the flight deck and call us here when you're ready.'

'Jesus!' Schulman groaned.

'Have a sandwich,' Captain Pancroft suggested.

'Thanks,' Schulman said. 'That's a thought. I mean, I like the high life.'

He grabbed a sandwich from the counter, jammed it into his mouth, started chewing and waved a hand in farewell as he walked out of the canteen. Dalton ordered more coffees and the man was quick in getting them. Dalton passed the cups around and they all sipped their coffee.

'You're pretty smart,' Dalton said.

'I hope so,' Masters replied.

'I know that's how you made it to the SBS, but you should come work for me. The pay's an awful lot better.'

'Don't tempt him, Paul,' Edwards said. 'We need him more than you do – and you'd just spoil him rotten.'

Pancroft looked at his watch. '0245 hours,' he said. 'Those boats should have set out from Peterhead by now. They'll be well on their way.'

'I hope so,' Dalton said.

'They'll be moving,' Edwards said. 'Major Lockyard is a very good man. He knows what he's doing.'

'I don't like it,' Pancroft said. 'I want to get out of here. I wish that young Yank pilot would get moving and pick up the telephone.'

'You take the maintenance men,' Edwards told him. 'You know all about that business. When we reach the deck, go straight to that pontoon leg and get them to fix up the hole.'

'I may not get there,' Pancroft replied.

'You'll be protected,' Masters assured him. 'I'll make sure you're covered all the way. I'll make sure you get there.'

'I want McGee,' Dalton said quietly.

'So do I,' Masters told him.

'I want him alive,' Dalton said. 'I want to talk to that bastard.'

'Who backed him?' Pancroft asked. 'I'd really like to know that. McGee . . . he must know.'

'That's right,' Dalton said. 'McGee knows. And we'll make sure he tells us.'

The telephone ran and the man behind the counter picked it up. He was hot and wiped sweat from his forehead as he put the phone down.

'The helicopter pad,' he said to Masters. 'They want you all up there.'

They left the canteen and climbed to the flight deck. The lights on the structures beamed down, cutting swathes through the darkness. Masters heard the wind moaning mournfully through the derricks; it was stronger than it had been before and that made him feel good. They all crossed the catwalk, where the wind was even stronger; it came from the north and blew straight across them, sweeping south. The sea was very far below, but obscured by the darkness; they could hear it smashing into the concrete legs as they passed over open space. Then they were on the landing pad, where the Dragonfly was already roaring, its rotors whipping the air about them as they hurried towards it. They bent low beneath the rotors, leaning into the slipstream. Two men in yellow overalls were pulling the blocks away from the wheels as the wind howled about them.

'You going as well, chief?' one of them asked Dalton.

'Yep.'

'You better get that suit off and put on some overalls,' the man said.

'I thought you'd never ask,' Dalton replied.

The man grinned and jerked his thumb towards the hut at the edge of the landing pad. As Edwards and Pancroft clambered up into the helicopter, Dalton hurried to the hut, remained inside for a few minutes, then emerged wearing a pair of orange overalls. To Masters's surprise, he also had a 9mm Browning High Power handgun holstered at the hip.

'I always carry one,' he explained without being asked. 'Even when I'm wearing my nice grey suit. It comes with the territory.'

Masters nodded and stood aside to let Dalton climb into the Dragonfly. When the American had done so, Masters followed him.

With its narrow fuselage, the Dragonfly wasn't

really suitable for four passengers, the pilot and a loadmaster, but they gamely squeezed in. As Schulman made his way to the pilot's cabin in the nose, the loadmaster slid the side door closed, then indicated that they should strap themselves in. Then, with Schulman at the controls, the Dragonfly roared even louder, shuddered violently, bounced a little and lifted off the ground. The deck fell far below them, a deeper darkness closed in, and then the Dragonfly lurched in the wind and headed towards the Beryl Field.

Masters looked out at the sky to see the moon lighting up the huge clouds. Glancing to his right, he saw the winking lights of Maureen, though he couldn't discern the oil rig itself. The Dragonfly rose and fell, roaring, shuddering, and swaying, fighting against the wind that was blowing fiercely down from the north, between Shetland and Norway. Masters was pleased to feel its buffeting; it was just what he wanted. Let the sea rise up and smash the whole bloody rig; let it provide the SBS with cover and distract the terrorists.

Schulman chewed gum ceaselessly and glanced keenly around him. Masters grinned at the sight of him, strangely comforted by the younger man's presence. He closed his eyes, put his head back on the seat and tried to let the time pass.

'What time is it?' Dalton asked.

'0430 hours,' Pancroft told him.

'What time do you think we'll get there?'

'About 0500 hours,' the captain said.

The time seemed to pass slowly. The helicopter bucked and roared, battered by the wind. Masters opened his eyes and glanced left to see lights far below. They were the lights of the Piper Field, winking fitfully in the darkness. Although Masters couldn't see the oil rigs, he knew the work was still going on there, twenty-four hours a day. He shifted uncomfortably in his narrow seat, watching the lights moving backwards, falling behind until nothing was left but darkness.

'What time is it?' Dalton asked again.

'0440 hours,' Pancroft told him.

'Jesus Christ,' Dalton said, 'we're in a black hole, with time running backwards.'

'We're nearly halfway there,' Schulman informed him.

'Good,' Dalton replied.

'It's a bitch of a night,' the pilot said. 'There's a storm coming up.'

They said nothing after that, concentrating on the sky outside, seeing only the moonlight rippling and gliding over clouds that were black painted on blackness. Schulman chewed his gum. Pancroft checked his watch. Dalton was lost deep in thought, his face hidden in shadow. The Dragonfly kept going, its roar filling their heads, shuddering and bucking more with each mile, battling against the growing wind. Masters emptied his mind. It was a trick he had learnt somewhere. He went down through himself to find peace, then slowly surfaced again. Opening his eyes, he glanced down and saw more lights, winking in the blackness far below.

'Beryl,' Schulman announced.

'Just keep going,' Masters told him.

'The rig's still afloat,' Schulman observed. 'You want me to take you lower to have a look?'

'No,' Edwards said. 'We have other fish to fry.'

They flew over Charlie 2, recognizable by its lights. Slowly those lights passed below and behind them and then the darkness returned. Schulman studied his chart, looking for the RV, then snapped his fingers and said: 'Here we go!' as he began his descent. They dropped to a thousand feet, passing through some thin clouds. Looking down, they saw nothing but darkness, a black abyss streaked with grey light. Schulman flew back and forth, circling around the void. He was looking for the lights of the boats, but so far there was nothing.

'We're too early,' Masters explained.

'I gathered that,' Schulman replied.

'Head direct for Lerwick,' Edwards said. 'We're bound to pass over them.'

The pilot did as he was told, keeping at low altitude. The Dragonfly rocked crazily, shuddered rapidly, then steadied again. Masters checked the sea below, but it was still lost in darkness. The clouds above had cut off the moonlight, and that would help the assault. Still, he kept looking, wanting to see those damn lights. If the lights didn't appear pretty soon, they'd be too far away. The Dragonfly growled and shook. A black mass passed overhead. The helicopter was fighting the wind and flying under the clouds. Another five minutes passed and then finally, far below and just ahead, they saw the moving lights of the SBS boats.

'There they are,' Schulman said.

'Thank Christ for that,' said Pancroft. 'I thought they might still be in Peterhead, bottled up by the storm.'

'I'm going down,' Schulman told them.

'Right,' Edwards said. 'Get down there and drop us on *Victory*. That should be the lead boat.'

As the Dragonfly dropped lower, the lights ahead raced towards them. The lights were like candles in a black room, appearing to float in space. Then they grew larger, illuminating the ploughing boats. There were five boats and they formed a large triangle with its tip pointing towards the Beryl Field. Schulman dropped lower, coming down over the lead boat. The Dragonfly dipped forward, rocking lightly, shuddering, but continuing its oblique, almost vertical descent until the boats could be made out in detail. Dimmed lights illuminated the sunken decks and their off-white submersibles.

'The first boat?' Schulman checked.

'The first one,' Edwards confirmed.

'OK,' Schulman said. 'We're right on top of it. I'm going down now.'

The Dragonfly started falling, in a perpendicular descent. As it did so it rocked wildly, shuddered more violently, and roared even louder against the howling wind. Masters looked down on *Victory*. The deck was expanding dramatically right below him, a pattern of dim light and shadow, rising up, then falling back again. As the Dragonfly hovered over the deck, swaying dangerously in the wind, the sea was whipped up by the slipstream and sloshed over the vessel. The waves were ribbons of black and white, forming circles around the boat. The circles rushed in to explode and soar skyward and then sweep out again. The submersible-carrier had dropped anchor and the Dragonfly stayed right above it, hovering about thirty feet above the deck, hammered by the fierce wind.

'Right, men,' Edwards said. 'Let's get down on that boat.'

Everyone except Schulman unclipped their safety belts and gathered around the sliding door in the side, where already the loadmaster was working at the lowering harness of the rescue winch. Satisfied, he slid the heavy door open, to let in a freezing wind that howled and pummelled at those gathered near the opening.

With a wave of his right hand the loadmaster indicated that the CO should put on the canvas harness. Experienced at this, Edwards did as he was told. He then sat in the doorway, his legs dangling over the side, and carefully let himself slide out. The straps went taut above him and then he was winched down, with the loadmaster controlling his rate of descent and Edwards controlling his own position in the battering slipstream.

Masters leant forward to look down. He saw Edwards swinging out on the slipstream, then back in the other direction in a dangerous arc. Nevertheless, he was going down, veering this way and that, bobbing up and down, spinning, but gradually shrinking as he descended over the boat. The wet deck dipped and climbed. The deck hands were looking up. Edwards swung right above them, still spinning in the slipstream. When he had dropped low enough, two pairs of hands reached up to pull him aboard.

Dalton went next, spiralling down into the darkness. He too was tossed to and fro by the wind, but he kept dropping steadily. Masters looked down as Dalton was grabbed and pulled aboard, the American releasing the straps and tugging three times to inform the loadmaster. The latter winched the harness back up, helped Pancroft into it, and lowered him down the same way. Then Masters put the harness on, sat in the wind-blown doorway, and heard the voice of his young friend Schulman.

'Don't get too wet down there!' Schulman called out. 'Don't go for a swim! Give me a call if you get back in one piece and I'll buy you a beer. *Adiós* and good luck!'

Masters dropped into space. The wind howled and picked him up and threw him sideways and then the straps took control of him. He dangled high above the boat, above the black sea and white foam, aware only of pale faces staring up from the darkness, squinting against the wind and spray as they checked his position. Then he was lowered down, swinging in and out on the wind, spinning, dizzy, fighting for breath, his head tight and filled with noise: the roaring helicopter, the howling wind, the squeaking winch, the pounding, splashing waves and the bawling of many men. The descent seemed to take a long time – as if time had stood still – but eventually two pairs of hands grabbed him and pulled him down to the boat.

He rolled across the deck, then stood shakily and released the harness. Looking up and blinking, rubbing salt water from his eyes, he saw Lieutenant-Colonel Edwards, Captain Pancroft, Dalton and a lot of soaked, grinning deck hands. The harness was winched up and pulled into the Dragonfly. The side door was slid shut. The helicopter ascended vertically, hovered shuddering for a moment, then headed back the way it had come, disappearing in darkness.

'Home and dry,' Lieutenant-Colonel Edwards said with a grin.

'Hardly dry,' Masters said.

15

Victory was tossing from side to side. The sea roared and smashed over it. The other submersible-carriers had stopped also and were widely spread out in a triangular formation, rising up and falling on the high waves. Masters fought to keep his balance as the icy spray showered over him. Looking around, he saw the lights of the other boats illuminating the water. The wind howled and made the sea hiss and swirl and then explode into fine white spray.

'That sea's rough,' Dalton said.

'It's only just starting,' Masters told him. 'I wouldn't like to see it in an hour. Those waves will be murder.'

The men on deck were a combination of Royal Navy sailors, divers and SBS Marine Commandos, all wearing wet suits. Lieutenant-Colonel Edwards and Captain Pancroft were already donning wet suits while talking to the CO's second in command, Major Laurence Lockyard, who had come from Peterhead on *Victory*. Six other men were on the lower deck at the stern, clambering over the four pinioned submersibles. The stern was open to the sea. A steel frame formed a bridge. The submersibles were connected to the frame, all set to be lowered. The stern rose and fell to let more waves wash over it. The men at the submersibles were in wet suits as black as the night.

'Are those the maintenance men?' Edwards asked Major Lockyard.

'Yes, boss. They've already put their kit and explosives in the submersibles, but they're waiting to talk to you.'

'Good,' Edwards said. He zipped up his wet suit and was starting forward when he was approached by a Royal Navy officer wearing a soaked gabardine raincoat over his uniform.

'Lieutenant-Colonel Edwards?'

'Yes.'

'I'm the captain of *Victory*. Lieutenant Commander William Sandison. Apart from being told to rendezvous here, I'm still a bit in the dark.'

'I want us dropped off in the submersibles at a given location, then your boats can return to Peterhead. You don't need to know any more than that. Where are we, precisely?'

'Ten miles east of Charlie 2. You said five, but you arrived too early. We only stopped to let you aboard. Shall I start up again?'

'Will the submersibles go that far?'

'A lot farther than that if you want.'

'Excellent. You can drop us off right now.'

Victory rose and fell, then a roaring wave drenched them. The water swept noisily around their feet and then poured out through drainage holes on both sides. Masters, slipping into his wet suit, as was Dalton, looked at the other four boats in the triangular formation. The reflections of their lights were dancing in the hollows between the waves, racing to and fro like flying saucers, gliding like fireflies.

'Are the men in the other boats ready?' Edwards asked Lockyard.

'They should be,' Lockyard replied. 'They won't be in the submersibles right now, but that can soon be arranged.'

'Weapons?'

'Full kit. L34A1s and Armalites with M203s, as requested. They're also equipped with Brownings, number 80 white-phosphorus incendiary grenades, a variety of plastic explosives, and abseiling equipment.'

'Our kit and weapons?'

'Already in the submersibles.'

'Instructions?'

'I deliberately left those vague, but told the men you would be filling them in when we left for the Beryl Field.'

'What do they know about Charlie 2?'

'Only that it's been captured and that they have to get it back. They know commencement time is 0600 hours, but they don't know much else.'

The CO looked at his watch. It was 0530 hours. They would have to leave very soon.

'Are they in contact?' he asked.

'All communications systems are open,' Lockyard informed him. 'Just give me the word.'

'Right,' Edwards said. 'I want the men in the submersibles as of right now. I want the submersibles launched straight away.'

'How do you do that?' Dalton asked Masters as Edwards went off to have words with the six-man maintenance team, now waiting patiently on top of a submersible on the low stern deck.

'It's pretty simple, though easier in better weather,' Masters told him. 'A large lift-line picks the submersible up off the deck and lowers it to just above the water. A diver stands on the casing and disconnects the lift-line to let the submersible half sink in the sea. It's held up by a tow-rope. We tow it out to its diving position and then, when it's all set to go, the diver disconnects the tow-rope. You sink to whatever depth you require and then switch on the engines. It's as simple as that.'

'What kind of submersibles are they?'

'Vickers Pisces III,' Masters said. 'Battery-operated.'

'Communications?'

'Marconi Modular systems with thruster control circuits, sub to sub. No interference at all.'

'So the boats pull away, we float on the end of tow-ropes, the CO gives his instructions while we're drifting and then we cast off.'

'Very good, Mr Dalton.'

Dalton grinned. 'Will we get there in half an hour?'

'Those little buggers are fast,' Masters said.

'I certainly hope so.'

They had to wait for five minutes until the CO returned from the lower deck. 'Right,' he said crisply. 'I've just given the maintenance team their instructions regarding the plugging of the hole blown in the pontoon leg by the terrorists, should such be the case. They're dividing into three teams, taking three of the four submersibles. You, Rudy,' he said to Captain Pancroft, 'will join the first team, then take command of all the teams once the assault begins. You, Mr Dalton, will be in the second and are responsible for yourself once aboard the rig.'

'That's as it should be,' Dalton said.

'I'll take the third submersible,' the CO continued. 'Major Lockyard will cross by motor launch to boat two, *Nelson*, and you, Sergeant Masters, will leave from this boat in the fourth submersible. Any questions, gentlemen?'

All the men grouped around the CO shook

their heads. The CO glanced at the other boats. The wind howled and the sea was roaring, with the waves curling higher each minute, exploding over the deck. The CO studied the sky. It was black and forbidding. Glancing across at the other four boats, he saw their lights through glistening showers of spray.

'I'll contact the others from *Nelson*,' Lockyard said, 'and order them into the submersibles. I'll have them all over the side fifteen minutes from now.'

The CO checked the time. 'Good. Let us drift for five minutes. That will give me enough time to brief the men. We can all cast off then.'

Lockyard nodded and went to the starboard side to catch the small launch that would take him to *Nelson*. The others made their way to the stern, being careful and holding firmly to the railings. The sea was roaring all around them, sweeping noisily across the deck, pouring over the other side or through the drainage holes while the ship rose and fell and plunged through more oncoming waves. They finally reached the submersibles. The maintenance men were already boarding. The launching deck resembled a cross-Channel ferry and the wind howled icily across it. The ship was rolling from side to side, the sea roared and flooded the deck, but the submersibles were pinioned firmly to their stays and, though drenched, seemed secure.

Twenty feet long and eleven feet high, the

miniature submarines looked like huge insects perched on skis. The ports comprised three round windows and had reinforced lights above them. On each side there were propellers. They had no rudders, but were steered simply by increasing the drive on the relevant propeller. Squat legs joined up to the skids, which were to allow movement on the seabed. Beneath the ports, at the base of the prow, was the manipulator assembly, or CAMS (Cybernetic Anthropomorphous Machine System): a set of robotic steel arms used for remote-control work on the seabed. It was those windows on the nose of the submersibles, Masters realized, combined with the skids, that made them look like giant insects.

As Edwards, Pancroft and Dalton were clambering into their respective submersibles, *Josephine*, *Huk* and *Genesis*, Masters looked up at the two muscular SBS corporals waiting on top of the fourth submersible, *Trinity*. Wind-blown and drenched, they had bandoliers of white-phosphorus incendiary grenades strung around their wet suits. The grenades were all wrapped tightly in cling film to protect them from the water. Masters didn't know the men. Both were specialists with all kinds of boats and in another squadron.

'Who's in charge?' Masters asked.

'I am,' one of the men, a blond giant, said.

'Do you know what you're here for?'

'No, Sarge.'

'It's terrorists,' Masters said. 'They've taken over Charlie 2 and threatened to blow a hole in a pontoon leg if we attack. Unfortunately, we have no choice, so we're going to attack. The job of this team is to mend the leg before the rig sinks.'

'We'll have to fight our way to it.'

'Correct,' Masters said. 'We three can take care of the fighting while Captain Pancroft leads the men down the pontoon leg. That's it. Let's go.'

Without a word, the second corporal clambered into the submersible and Masters followed him in, first grabbing hold of its curved metal 'sail' to haul himself up. Once on top, he had to fight to keep his balance, since the boat was now rocking heavily. Waiting for the first man to lower himself down the hatch, Masters glanced at the boat's low, open stern and saw a powerful wave breaking over it, filling the air with a fountain of hissing spray. The corporal dropped through the hatch, then disappeared completely, so Masters swung his legs over, sat briefly on the edge of the steel sail, then carefully lowered himself down.

He landed on a wooden deck. Beneath the deck were pipes and pumps. The interior of the submersible was small and very cramped, with curved walls of steel and a low ceiling. Masters had to stoop low. The hatch was directly above his head. He saw two curved wooden benches around the side of the sphere, facing the three ports at the front. There was more equipment beneath the benches, there were controls on all sides, and every available space in the sphere was covered with gauges and valves.

The corporal was at the pilot's console, sitting on a low wooden bench. When a pair of big, soaked boots dropped down just above Masters's head, he had to quickly move back. Bumping his head on the low ceiling, he cursed and sat on the bench. The blond giant had just dropped on to the wooden deck and was shutting the hatch. He grunted as he turned the locking wheel, which made a harsh, grating sound. The noise reverberated around the small sphere and then the wheel clicked shut. The blond giant muttered something and knelt between the benches. He seemed ridiculously large in that enclosed space, grinning at Masters.

'They're pretty small,' he said.

'Too small,' Masters replied.

'I don't like to be underwater in these fuckers. At least not for long.'

Suddenly, the submersible started shaking and giving off reverberating metallic sounds. Startled, Masters glanced up, then he recognized the sound of clanging chains.

'It's the diver,' the blond giant explained. 'He's standing on top of the submersible. He'll stay there while we're lowered over the stern and then he'll disconnect the lift-line. The boat will pull away from us and we'll float out on the tow-rope. Then, when we're ready to cast off, he'll disconnect that as well.'

The man's voice had an echo, as did every sound inside the sphere. The lights were on and they shone down the curved walls, gleaming off pipes and valves. Masters didn't feel claustrophobic – he'd been well trained for this – but he certainly felt the urge to get out and back into the open air. Trying to distract himself, he glanced around the cramped sphere. The corporal-pilot was facing the pilot's console, checking gauges and dials. Masters glanced at his watch. It was 0540 hours. They would reach the rig shortly after 0600 hours, which is when it would all start.

The submersible started vibrating, shaking violently, breaking loose, then it jumped up and swung from side to side as if hanging in space. That's exactly what was happening: it was swinging over the launching deck. It had been picked up by the lift-line and was now swinging over the stormy sea. Masters held on to the bench, feeling a bit disorientated. The submersible shook with a dreadful clanging sound, then suddenly dropped like a stone, going down very fast. There was a crashing sound as the dropping motion stopped abruptly, followed by a reverberating drumming sound as the submersible bounced up and down and finally settled again, rocking lightly from side to side.

'We're drifting out,' the corporal said. 'The boat's pulling away. When we stop drifting out, the tow-rope's tight. We get the CO's speech then.'

Masters gazed through a porthole. The sea fell away into darkness. The waves rolled up and rushed down to form a tunnel, then raced up again. The sea was extremely rough, and it was like being on a big dipper. Masters felt his stomach heave as they climbed up and then plunged down again.

Outside the porthole was a whirlpool of water; rushing forward, it smashed noisily against the port, swirled around wildly as if in a washing machine, then fell away to reveal the dark sky, drifting clouds, a few stars. This movement was continuous and soon became sickening, with the submersible leaning over dramatically, then straightening again.

Masters crawled away from the porthole and sat on the wooden bench, but instantly was almost thrown sideways by another violent motion. He heard the drumming of the sea against the hull, then the sphere settled down.

Turned on by the corporal, the radio was crackling. The voice of Lieutenant Commander Sandison came through the speaker, distorted and unreal. '*Victory* to *Josephine*. *Victory* to *Josephine*. You are now in position to tow-drift. We will launch in five minutes.'

'*Josephine* to *Victory*. *Josephine* to *Victory*. Message received. Roger and out.'

The corporal turned around. He had left the radio open. Waving his right hand at the console, he nodded to Masters.

'The CO should come on any minute now, then we'll be taking off. The CO's in *Josephine*.'

'*Josephine* to all subs. *Josephine* to all subs,' came over the radio. 'This is your Commanding Officer speaking. We are now in tow-drift and will be casting off as soon as I finish speaking. We will be heading for Charlie 2. That rig has been hijacked. The crew have all been murdered and sixty terrorists are now aboard. We have to rout the terrorists and take the rig back. We are not concerned with damage to the rig, nor with the lives of the terrorists. Once aboard you will shoot to kill. You will board by climbing the pontoon legs. Your orders are to commence firing as soon as you reach the deck or as soon as the enemy fires. We are casting off now. We will submerge to three hundred feet. We will follow the chart route to Charlie 2 and surface under the main deck. The pilots will open the hatches and check with the other pilots. No one is to move to the ladders until all hatches are open. There's to be no noise down there. The assault commences when *Josephine* signals. At the signal you will advance to the ladders with weapons ready to fire. Select the ladder closest to you. Shoot on sight of the enemy. Don't stop until the whole rig is cleared and every terrorist is either dead or captured. Over and out.'

When the static rushed back in the corporal turned the volume down. He turned the volume back up a few seconds later, when the CO came back on line.

'Instructions for *Auk*, *Huk* and *Genesis*. Repeat: instructions for *Auk*, *Huk* and *Genesis*. You are not to engage the enemy unless absolutely necessary. Your mission is to get to the damaged pontoon leg. You will stay with the crew of *Trinity*, who will give you cover. You will descend into the damaged pontoon leg and repair it as best you can. Take full diving kit and wet-welding equipment. As you also have to carry the replacement plates for the pontoon leg, the only weapons you can carry are your Brownings. Repeat: stick with *Trinity*. Your mission is to fix that damaged leg. I want no deviations.'

Masters checked his watch. It was 0550 hours. They would get to Charlie 2 by 0630. It would still be dark then.

'We're casting off now,' the CO announced over the radio. 'Good luck to all of you. Over and out.'

When the corporal switched off the radio, Masters stared around the sphere. The walls curved upward to meet above his head where a bright light was blazing. They were covered in gauges, the benches hid more equipment, and the spaces between the floorboards of the deck were filled with steel pipes and pumps. Masters blinked a few times, heard the drumming of the sea, looked at the three small, round windows and saw the dark waves outside. Then he heard the diver's footsteps as he walked along the hull. There was a dull metallic sound from the stern as the tow-rope dropped off. This was followed by splashing and a scraping along the hull. The diver's face, grotesque in his oxygen mask, appeared at the window. He stuck up one thumb. The pilot waved back. A white foam bubbled over the window as the diver swam off.

The pilot switched on the engines, which made a bass humming sound. When he switched on the outside lamps their light beamed into the dark waves. The pilot opened the vents and water hissed into the tanks; the sea rose up above the three portholes and gradually covered them. The submersible sank steadily, vibrating and humming deeply. Masters went to a porthole and looked out and saw the murky, deceptive depths. The beams of light cut about six or seven feet through the gloom. It was not very far; beyond the lights was total darkness. The only matter lit up by the dulled beams of the lamps was a drifting, grey-green mass.

The depth gauge registered a hundred feet, inched

around to two hundred, and after what seemed like a long time finally registered three hundred. The pilot closed the vents, then turned on the radio. He checked that the other submersibles were all down and then turned the propellers on.

The submersible moved forward, its lights cutting through the murk. The vessel vibrated slightly, making a bass humming sound, and the hands on all the gauges were quivering, recording their progress. The pilot switched on the sonar set. After studying the small screen, he checked the gyro compass and settled back, keeping his eye on the lights through the windows.

'What's your name?' Masters asked him.

'Walters. Roy Walters.'

'And you?' Masters asked the blond giant.

'Ralph Hubbert.'

Masters couldn't stand upright, could scarcely move his arms; it was more comfortable sitting, so he sat there and studied the weapons. There were L34A1 Sterling 9mm sub-machine-guns and twenty-round magazines, all wrapped in specially reinforced cling film. He also saw a pile of white-phosphorus grenades, some police clubs, sets of handcuffs, and, to his relief, a couple of Browning 9mm High Power handguns, also wrapped in cling film, as were the holsters.

'We've been well equipped,' he said, picking up a holstered Browning and strapping it, still wrapped in its cling film, around the waist of his wet suit.

'That's what you wanted, wasn't it?' Hubbert said.

'That's right,' replied Masters. 'I got just what I wanted.'

Hubbert grinned laconically. He was sitting on the bench facing Masters, his blond head almost scraping the convex ceiling, his large hands on his thick thighs.

'You think we'll get them?' he asked.

'We've *got* to get them,' Masters told him.

'They're a tough nut to crack,' Hubbert said. 'The IRA, they're all psychos.'

'You think so?' Masters asked.

'Yeah, I think so. They're all psychos and fucking suicidal. It's part of their rules.'

'You've been in Northern Ireland?'

'Nah,' Hubbert said. 'I haven't fought them, but I've read all about them and they're all mad as hatters.'

Masters said nothing.

The voyage seemed to take for ever. They were gliding through silence. The submersible was vibrating and humming, but it moved forward smoothly. Masters went up to the front, where he heard the pinging of the sonar; he saw the pinpoints of light on the screen and the beams of light outside, cutting through the dark sea. The darkness parted where the light shone, then spread its wings around them. The beams lit up translucent fish through the murk. Masters could almost hear the silence out there, feel the cold of the sunless depths. He sat beside the pilot, who was still watching the gyro compass. The needle of the compass was quivering, but moved very little.

'How long?' Masters asked.

'About ten minutes,' Walters said. 'We'll have to start surfacing in five minutes. I think the sea's pretty rough.'

'How rough?' Masters asked.

'Bloody rough, Sarge. Those waves might be fifty foot high. I can't be sure, but they could be.'

'The rig?' Masters asked.

'The rig's out,' Walters said. 'If we try to get under that bloody rig, we'll be smashed to pieces.'

'We'll have to surface,' Masters said.

'That's right: we'll have to surface. We'll have to come up well away from the rig and then put on our diving masks.'

'That's not practical, Corporal.'

'Yes, it is, Sarge. We'll keep our weapons in cling film, put them in a sealed bag, then drag the buggers behind us in the bag. No problem at all.'

'What about the replacement plates? That crew can't drag them through the water – they're too heavy.'

'No,' Walters said, 'they won't be able to take the plates with them – but they *will* be able to take the welding equipment and that could be enough. Failing that, though it'll take a bit more time, they'll find plates on the rig.'

Masters swallowed hard as he thought of fifty-foot waves, imagining the men swimming through the water, beneath the sea's killing surface. They would come up under the pontoons, at the base of their huge legs. They would climb the pontoon ladders to the surface and the waves would then find them. In waves like that, the men would have to be strong. Doubtless more than one man would be lost before he reached the top deck.

'OK,' Masters said, 'I take your point. So let's see if the CO agrees. Give me that microphone.'

When Walters handed him the microphone, Masters contacted *Josephine*. He asked for the CO and, when he got him, relayed the corporal's theory to him. To his credit, Lieutenant-Colonel Edwards instantly agreed, saying he would instruct the other submersibles to surface right now, on the present grid reference.

'Thank Corporal Walters for me,' he added. 'He must be a bright boy. Over and out.'

Masters handed the microphone back to Walters. 'You're a bright boy,' he said.

'Can we surface right now?' Walters asked, as if not quite believing in his own wisdom.

'Right now,' Masters said.

Walters opened the tanks and the deep humming changed pitch slightly. Masters heard the tanks ejecting their water and then the craft started rising.

'Bless us all,' Walters said.

Hubbert slid off the bench, pulled some rubber bags from out under it, and passed one each to Masters and Walters. Each man then placed his weapons and other kit in his rubber bag, zipped it up, sealed it with water-resistant tape, then slung it on to his back and tightened the shoulder straps.

'Well,' Masters said, 'it's a start.'

As it rose slowly from the depths, the submersible started to rock from side to side. Hubbert sat on the bench beside Masters and gripped the arm-rest. Masters glanced through the portholes and saw light outside. The separate beams of light were rising up and down, splaying wide, disappearing. The submersible kept rising, rocking more as it neared the surface, and Masters heard the drumming noise from outside as the waves grew in strength.

'Right,' Hubbert said. 'Here we go. Help me on with the cylinders.'

After putting on his flippers, he knelt by the bench and told Masters to hold up the heavy oxygen cylinders. When Masters had done this, Hubbert put his hands backwards through the straps, then humped the cylinders on to his broad back. Masters then buckled the straps around his chest and Hubbert put on his oxygen mask. When he had finished, he nodded at Masters and held up his thumb.

The submersible was still rising and rocking more rapidly; it was coming to the surface and it was stormy up there. Masters put on his flippers and picked up his oxygen cylinders, but Hubbert stepped forward, walking awkwardly on his own flippers, and helped Masters put on his cylinders. Masters then covered his face with the oxygen mask, instantly feeling hot and suffocated, as well as half blind. He clipped the breathing tube in and turned around to look at Hubbert. They gazed at one another through their masks, then turned on the oxygen.

The submersible was still lurching badly from side to side. Masters turned around and blinked through his mask and saw Walters sitting at the console, putting on his flippers. When he had done so, he stood up and reached for his cylinders. Hubbert helped him to put them on, though both were shaken by the submersible, which was rocking more violently all the time as it rose to the surface. Masters watched the two men. They both moved in total silence. The only sound Masters heard was his own breathing, the rhythmic hiss of the oxygen. Finally Walters was ready, and pressed his hands against the wall. Hubbert followed his example, so Masters did the same and then waited.

The submersible broke the surface. It soared up and crashed back down. It was swept along the trough between waves and then hurled up again. Masters timed the rise and fall, bracing himself beneath the hatch. The submersible raced along the next trough and Masters reached up above him. He turned the wheel very hard, wrenching with all his might. The submersible reached the crest of a wave and started racing back down again. Masters wrenched the hatch open, grabbed the handles on both sides, held on as the submersible plummeted down and spun around and rushed sideways. It ascended again, climbing a huge wave; and Masters took a deep breath and jerked his arms and pulled himself up.

He flopped over the curved steel sail. A monstrous wave towered above him. It roared and then curled above his head, before exploding all over him. Masters clung to the sail as the water swirled around him. When it poured back down the sides of the submersible, the wind started beating. The noise was incredible – Masters heard it through his mask. He glanced up and saw the sea's rise and fall, the huge waves heaving skyward. Masters clambered over the sail and took the grip in one hand. He reached down with his other hand to let Hubbert reach up and take hold of it. Masters started pulling.

A wave picked the submersible up. Masters felt the wind and heard the roaring wave and saw a valley of darkness. The water down there was black. It poured away and swept up again. Masters held the grip tight as the submersible plunged down and then was borne up on another high wave. He tried not to look around him, tried ignoring the roaring sea. Taking a deep breath, he pulled Hubbert up and knew that Walters was pushing him. Hubbert flopped across the sail, wriggled around and lay flat out. He took hold of the other grip, then he and Masters started reaching down for Walters. The sea roared and swept across them, sweeping Hubbert off the hull; then the submersible rose high on a great wave and Masters flew into empty space.

He didn't know what was happening, but saw distant lights spinning, a huge wall of darkness rising high to block out the sea and sky. Then there was the void, streams of light through a blackness, and he kept spinning, turning rapidly upside down, bereft of any sense of direction. His head broke the surface as he rose on a roaring wave. He saw the lights of the rig straight ahead, soaring up to the sky. It didn't seem real, was too fierce to be real. He was carried through the air, felt the wind, and then was hurled down again.

At that moment Masters sensed that he wouldn't come back up. He saw a submersible spinning around not far away, then dark forms in the monstrous waves. Masters blinked and glanced below. He saw a black, concave void. He was plunging rapidly towards it and it roared and then swallowed him whole.

16

Masters didn't rise up again. He kicked out with his flippers and went down, gliding through the dark, silent depths to where the waves could not reach him. A grey-green murk filled his vision, he felt as light as a feather, and he went down, levelled out and kicked his legs, heading straight for the rig.

There were other men around him in the calm and quiet, looking like strange, primordial fish, but kicking their legs and blowing bubbles, dragging bags on long chains. Masters was thrilled to see them, and proud too.

He saw the shadows increasing in number in the murk all around him, and coming closer. A lot of the men had obviously made it. That was due to their training. They were now swimming expertly all around him and still had their weapons, some in waterproof bags strapped to their shoulders, others in bags that they towed behind them on short, lightweight chains. Masters kicked harder and glided forward, hearing a hissing in his ears. It was the soft, rhythmic hissing of the oxygen, which was all he could hear. He glanced left and right, seeing streams of small bubbles, streaming back and upwards in silence, a dance of air and trapped light.

Masters felt divorced from his own body; apart from his own steady breathing, he could not hear a sound. The gloom ahead was unrelieved. Beyond it was total darkness which swallowed up the men ahead, the drifting bags, the kicking flippers. Masters headed straight for it, but it always moved on; the gloom parted and swept by on either side and the darkness receded. Nevertheless, he swam towards it, mesmerized by the silence. He started dreaming, drifting out of himself . . . and then he saw something moving.

Masters swam forward cautiously and approached shadowy figures. He saw a black wall that was darker than the depths, and the shadows were touching it. Masters swam on, gratefully breathing the oxygen, and the black wall became the immense bulk of the round pontoon.

He went into that darkness. The other men were spiralling above him, below him, beside him, vague figures drifting up and down languidly. Masters swam even closer until the pontoon curved above him. He went under it and swam around it and then went up towards the surface. He saw the base of the pontoon leg, still obscured by the murk. At least thirty feet wide, it dwarfed the swimming men, soaring above them to disappear into darkness. Masters swam close and touched it. A pair of flippers kicked above him. He glanced up and saw the bottom of the ladder, stopping short at the pontoon.

Masters took hold of a rung and started pulling himself up. It was difficult, so he took off his flippers and used his bare feet. The water was so icy his feet started turning numb within seconds; even so, other men were doing the same and discarded flippers drifted down past him.

Masters pulled himself up, trying not to go too fast. He knew that he would have to be holding the ladder when he broke through the surface. He kept moving upwards and saw the kicking feet above him; the water, cold and black, moved around him, filled with bubbles of trapped light. Masters heard his own harsh breathing, felt the tugging of the sea. The darkness weakened and let in some light and then the black became grey. Masters felt a sudden tension, but it passed away as he kept rising. He felt the swirling of that grey, icy mass and then he broke through the surface.

The noise exploded around him. He gripped the rung of the ladder. The sea roared and swept between the pontoon legs and then roared out again. Masters clung to the ladder, seeing men on the other pontoon legs. There were also men on the thinner support legs criss-crossing above him. The noise was appalling. The sea roared and hammered the great pontoon legs, exploding and shooting upwards and outwards, then pouring back down the support legs.

Masters gripped the ladder tightly as waves roared and swept across him. He was punched by the fist of a giant and nearly torn from the ladder. He clung desperately to the rung and watched the men on the support legs; they had jumars – metal clamps – attached to their belts and were fixing them to the rungs of the ladders. The jumars kept them from falling off, leaving their hands free for manoeuvring. Clamped tight to the rungs of the ladders, the men were helping each other. The sea roared and exploded, echoing under the deck above.

The men were now opening their waterproof bags and taking out their weapons. They slung the Sterlings across their backs, and clipped grenades to their webbed belts. The spare magazines were in small, waterproof bags that hung from loops around their necks. Masters climbed up the ladder, then stretched out on a support leg. He took a jumar that was chained to his waist belt and clamped it over a rung. The sea roared and swept across him, almost tearing him from the leg. Though only six inches long, the chain on the jumar kept him from being swept away. The sea came in once more, its white foam streaked with black, roaring up and clawing frantically at the men and then rushing back out again.

With their weapons at the ready, the men were starting the real climb, snapping the jumars open and clambering up the ladders and then locking the jumars around the nearest rung when they had to rest or use their hands for something else. The sea roared and swept across them, making some of them disappear. The sea rushed away and took the men with it, leaving no trace at all. The other men kept climbing, only stopping to help each other. Masters saw them disappearing in the darkness, climbing up to the main deck.

Suddenly kicked on the shoulder, he glanced along the support leg. The sea roared and poured across him to drench him, then he saw a pale face. Captain Pancroft was shouting at him, pointing at his back, telling him to remove his sub-machine-gun from his waterproof bag and have it ready for use when they boarded. He did as he was told, removing the weapon from the bag, slinging it across his shoulder, then attaching the spare magazines to his webbing – all while lying stretched out on the support leg, whipped by wind and lashed by rain. When he had finished, he waved to Pancroft, then snapped the jumar open. The demented sea rushed at him, making him cling to the support leg. The sea pummelled him and poured all around him and then fell away. He slithered back down the leg to reach the main pontoon leg, stretching out with one hand and taking hold and then swinging across. He landed on the other ladder as the waves roared in. Fifty feet high, they towered darkly above Masters, and made an indescribable noise as they exploded around him. He clung to the ladder, feeling the jolting along his arms, as the waves howled past and rushed beneath the rig and poured out through the other side.

Masters started climbing, but he had to rest often. When he did so, he used the jumar, snapping it over the nearest rung. The other men were all around him, above him and below him, clambering up the ladders of the pontoon legs, stretching along the support legs. They were vague in the gloom, but clearly fighting the fierce sea, using the short breaks between incoming waves to climb higher. Sometimes they failed, clamping themselves on too late; when this happened the waves smashing down upon them bore them away. Yet the other men kept climbing, advancing up into the gloom. They were swallowed by the darkness beneath the deck that loomed high above Masters.

He, too, kept climbing, fighting the wind and fierce sea. Though now well above the waves, he still felt the icy sting of the spray. The men above were near the deck, disappearing into darkness. Masters wondered if the first men were aboard, and if so, what was happening. The storm had grown extremely violent, making the rig sway and creak, and Masters hoped that the terrorists would be indoors, hiding from its fury. He kept climbing the ladder, the wind howling and teasing at him. The waves thundered below and the spray geysered up to him and drenched him.

Glancing back down the leg he saw men on the support legs, throwing off their cylinders and masks, unwrapping weapons and magazines. He also saw the snarling waves crashing over the swarming men, then rushing away, allowing the men to keep moving upwards, dark ants on a silvery web. Some crawled along the support legs; others climbed the great pontoon legs. They all climbed out of that roaring dark pit to clamber up the steel ladders.

Masters looked up again, to where the bottom of the main deck was spread out directly above him. Very close to him, it was swaying up and down, its bolts and nuts squealing in protest. Then Masters heard gunfire. It was coming from the main deck. It was the sound of Sterling sub-machine-guns, dominating the howling wind.

Masters reached the catwalk. It was dark and the wind howled across it, making it shudder and rattle. The sound of gunfire was now louder, rising above the howling wind, and the catwalk was moving up and down as the massive deck heaved. Masters reached up through the hatchway, grabbed the handles on either side, took a deep breath and pulled himself up and then rolled on the deck.

The wind beat about him, the sea roared and hissed below, and he glanced down to see foam-capped waves, climbing high, smashing in. More shots rang out. There was a muffled, deep explosion. Masters felt the blast jolting up his legs as he grabbed for the railing. He glanced down the pontoon leg. The sea was boiling around it. Someone screamed and was grabbed by a white claw and dragged into the darkness. The whole leg shook visibly, then the massive platform tilted. The seething water fell back and gave way to monstrous waves. Masters realized that the explosives had gone off in the pontoon leg and that he was now standing right on top of it as the water poured into it.

Cursing, shaking his head, he ran along the catwalk. He removed his Sterling from his shoulder as he ran, and managed to snap in a magazine just before he arrived at a ladder that climbed the wall of a module. He clambered up the ladder, using only his free hand; he reached the top and went through an open door where a bright light washed over him. He was on the drilling floor, right behind the stacked crates. The noise of gunfire echoed noisily and he saw other SBS men in wet suits. They were kneeling behind the crates, firing into the drilling room, and Masters looked beyond the crates and saw the terrorists, racing back and forth, shouting. They seemed small and distant. The drilling floor was very bright, its light falling across the crates and machines, casting large, bizarre shadows.

Masters knelt beside his friends and released the safety-catch on his Sterling. There was a roaring from the far side of the deck and wood splintered near his face. He and the others returned fire and the noise was harsh, almost deafening. A terrorist screamed and threw up his arms, then turned away and collapsed.

'Masters!' someone bawled. 'Over here!'

Jerking his head around, Masters saw Pancroft kneeling near the door. The captain still had his oxygen cylinders and breathing mask on, the latter strapped to his belt. Masters ran over to him as the guns roared right behind Pancroft. Dropping to a crouching position, Masters moved up beside him.

'They've blown the leg right beneath us,' Pancroft told him. 'That saves us a journey.'

'I know,' Masters replied. 'Where are the maintenance men?'

'Four are still making their way up to the deck, but I've got the first two just outside. That's all we need, Tone.'

The guns continued firing, someone screamed and fell down, and more SBS men were rushing through the open door, crouching low, weapons ready. Masters glanced back at the crates to see an SBS commando hurling a smoke grenade; he jumped up and his arm swung in a blur, then he dropped low again. The grenade flew far out above the drilling floor, seemed to hover there eternally, then dropped languidly towards the drilling room. The explosion came immediately, a cataclysmic roaring, with pieces of debris flying out on billowing smoke and men screaming inside.

'. . . the leg!' Pancroft was shouting as the smoke from the grenade thinned out. 'We've got to repair that pontoon leg! Come on, Sergeant! Let's go!'

Masters looked past the crates at the massive drilling floor, where SBS men were running, dropping low, then jumping up again. They were firing on the move and their fire was being returned. A terrorist hand-grenade exploded with a mighty roar and blew apart a large wooden crate. The smoke cleared to reveal a man writhing on the deck, screaming dementedly, his hands clawing at his lacerated, bleeding stomach. As he was wearing a wet suit, he had to be an SBS man, so another SBS man rushed up to him, intending to help him. A hail of bullets cut him down. His weapon clattered to the deck as he shuddered violently and then fell and rolled over, staring up at the sky. An SBS grenade exploded very close to the moonpool. Metal shrieked and a standpipe buckled and crashed down on some terrorists. Instantly, the SBS men in wet suits ran forward, firing from the hip, their guns roaring on both sides as the shouting of the men echoed noisily.

'Now!' Pancroft yelled, slapping Masters on the shoulder. They both jumped up and rushed through the doorway and felt the blast of the wind. Masters ran along the catwalk and saw the floor-hatch opening. The head of a terrorist emerged and the man looked up, startled. Masters glimpsed the wide eyes, that brief, scalding panic, then kicked the man's head, which jerked back and thumped on the catwalk. The terrorist vomited and dropped back through the hatch, leaving blood on the catwalk.

Masters dropped to his knees and looked down the pontoon leg. Something splashed far below – the body of the man he'd kicked – and then he saw another face staring up at him. The man was hanging from the ladder. The water boiled far below him. He glanced up and shouted 'No!' and Masters fired and saw blood and stripped bone. The man's face split in two, his hands slid from the ladder, his body curved back like a bowstring and his arms wildly waved, then he plunged down the dark, hollow leg and splashed into the water. Masters had another look. There was no sign of other terrorists. He glanced up and saw Pancroft with two SBS corporals, both wearing full diving kit.

'We're OK,' Masters told them. 'I know this rig well. There are spare plates on the catwalk in the leg. I don't think there's a problem.'

'Good,' Pancroft replied. 'These men have the welding kit and tools, so let's get the hell down there.'

Pancroft shuffled across the catwalk, his flippers around his neck. He untied them and put them on his feet and then untied the oxygen mask. The catwalk rose and fell, the wind howled, the sea roared. They heard the sound of gunfire from inside and then heard more above them. Pancroft put on his oxygen mask and waved at the two corporals. Encased in full diving equipment, they moved forward awkwardly. One of them had the welding kit in the bag on his back; the other was holding a battery-operated electric hammer and other bits of equipment.

Suddenly, the rig tilted farther and the pontoon leg sank lower. Thus reminded that time was running out, Pancroft sat on the edge of the hatch and then slid down and disappeared.

The second man took the same position. Masters heard a sound behind him. Turning to face the door, he saw a silhouette framed in light . . . and the barrel of an MP5 pointing straight at him. Masters fired first, moving his Sterling sub-machine-sun left to right, and as the weapon roared the terrorist shuddered wildly and fell back through the doorway. Another terrorist appeared. Masters shot him and he fell. Masters tugged a grenade from his belt and then ran to the door. After throwing in the grenade, he flattened himself against the wall; the grenade exploded and the steel wall vibrated. Masters rushed in.

One man was sliding down the crates, leaving a trail of blood behind him; another was rolling on the floor with his tattered clothes smoking; and the third was staggering blindly in circles, screaming in agony and fear, covering his blinded eyes with his bloody hands.

Masters's Sterling spat fire and he felt the backblast. The three men convulsed in a hail of bullets, then collapsed and were still.

Rushing back out to the hatchway in the catwalk, Masters looked in and saw the three SBS men on the ladder, climbing down towards the water. That water was far below them, over a hundred feet down, boiling up and sinking repeatedly, rushing in from outside and pouring out again. Masters closed the trapdoor, then checked the wind and sea. The storm was not as strong as it had been; it was gradually fading. He looked all around him, seeing grey light in the darkness, then turned away and went back through the doorway and into the drilling hall.

The dead men lay at his feet. Blood streaked the crates; Masters walked past these and looked out at the vast drilling floor. The SBS were still fighting and had reached the moonpool, where they were hiding behind the stacked pipes and chains, firing up at the drilling room. Masters ran across the floor, his bare feet slipping in mud; he was drenched and felt very cold, though there was sweat on his brow. The guns roared and bullets whistled, ricocheting on all sides. He kept running and on reaching a fork-lift dropped low behind it.

Bullets whipped past his head and a grenade exploded. Glass shattered and he heard a piercing scream that made him glance towards the moon-pool. His mates were stretched out around it, hiding behind what they could find, shouting at each other and waving arms and firing up at the drilling room. Masters looked at the room and saw terrorists at the windows. The glass was shattered and the terrorists were firing down at the men in wet suits. Then a grenade sailed towards the window and fell among the terrorists. When it erupted in a blinding flash of light, more shards of glass rained down.

The SBS men darted forward. A terrorist flopped through the smashed window. The SBS men raced across the floor, firing on the move, then ran up the stairs and turned a sharp corner, disappearing from view. Masters jumped up and ran, then saw a terrorist at the window, taking aim with an AK47, its barrel pointing at him. Before the terrorist could fire, someone shot him from behind. The terrorist was punched forward, over the window frame, then slid off and plunged screaming to the drilling floor. Relieved, Masters ran up the steps and turned into the drilling room. The other SBS troops were there, examining their own handiwork. The room was wrecked and the terrorists, all dead, were drenched in blood.

'Anyone seen Dalton?' Masters asked.

'Who's Dalton?' came the reply. 'If he's in a wet suit he's one of us. If not, he's in trouble.'

Masters left the drilling room and hurried along a narrow corridor; the lights were bright and the ceiling was low and he felt his eyes stinging. It was quiet in the corridor. Now the gunfire sounded distant. He kept walking and turned a sharp corner and then came to more steps. Catching a glimpse of blue overalls, he raised his weapon and fired a short burst. The overalls flapped like a wind-blown flag and then the man in them started falling. His weapon clattered down the steps and he pitched forward and followed it. His head thumped on a step and split open as his body flipped over. His boots banged on the floor, his spine cracked on another step, and then he sprawled there, propped up by the steps, as Masters jumped over him.

Masters raced up to the main deck and stepped out into the wind. He noticed that the storm had abated, though the wind was still icy. The sound of gunfire was loud here; it ricocheted and reverberated. There were men running this way and that, through shadow and light. A grenade exploded, its flash illuminating the darkness. Silhouetted figures spun in white light and crashed back down through boiling smoke.

The immense deck was tilting. It was covered in mud and oil. The guns roared and men shouted as they ran to and fro, exposed in bright lights, lost in shadows, skidding over the deck.

Masters glimpsed the sea far below the tilting deck, brief flashes of white through the gloom, a black void turning grey. Then he heard a shocking noise, felt fierce heat, was rendered breathless. Snatched up by a giant hand, he was smashed against a wall, blacked out for a moment, then awakened lying flat on his back. Looking straight up, he saw a towering derrick with lights blazing on its platforms. There was a scream and then he saw a man fall from a platform and plunge down through the moonpool to the sea.

Masters jumped up and advanced, still gripping his Sterling, glancing sideways at the base of the platform and expecting to die. He saw terrorists huddled up within the web of the girders, firing down from the roof of the drilling floor, their guns winking and chattering. Masters ran across the deck, trying to avoid the hail of bullets. A man in overalls jumped out from behind a wooden crate, aiming at him with a Glock 17 semi-automatic pistol.

The terrorist didn't have time to shoot: Masters just bowled right into him. They both tumbled to the deck and rolled over, one on top of the other. The man straightened up, still trying to aim his handgun, but Masters kicked his kneecap and he collapsed, his head thumping the steel deck. Then Masters jumped up. The man was rolling away from him. Masters took a step forward and kicked him in the ribs and on the head. The terrorist grunted and shuddered. Masters kicked his head again. There was a muffled snapping sound and the man twitched convulsively, then froze. Masters picked up his weapon as splinters of wood from the crates beside him exploded just above him. He turned away and ran as fast as he could toward the nearest derrick.

The other SBS troops were scattered widely around the deck, firing up at the derrick. The base of the derrick rested on the roof of the drilling room and the terrorists were firing down from there. The SBS troops were trying to storm it, rushing forward and dropping low. A CS gas grenade had fallen near the room and its smoke spiralled skyward. The sky itself was turning grey, drifting beyond the tall derrick, as the guns roared, a hand-grenade exploded and some SBS men screamed and fell.

Masters saw Corporal Hubbert pointing up at the shooting terrorists, drenched like the rest of the SBS men, his pale face now flushed. Masters crouched low and ran, but skidded crazily in the mud; he fell down and slithered over the deck and then crawled up to Hubbert. The blond giant stared at him. He seemed startled, but then he grinned as he poked a finger in his right ear, turned it like a corkscrew and gently smacked his own head.

'I'm half deaf!' he bawled.

'What happened to Walters?' Masters bawled back.

'I don't know! I haven't seen him since the climb! I don't think he made it!'

There was another loud explosion. Lumps of metal flew through the air, and a man's head bounced across the deck, pumping blood. Then Masters saw the body. It was standing beside some gas pipes, dressed in a shredded SBS wet suit, also pumping blood from its headless neck. One hand flapped in the air, the legs shook and then the body collapsed. Another explosion was followed by flying shrapnel. The guns of both sides roared in a dreadful cacophony.

'Those bastards!' Hubbert bawled. 'They're holed up in that bloody roof! There's nowhere they can go, so they're staying there and cutting us to pieces!' Suddenly, he stood up, fully exposed to the terrorists; he glanced at the men all around him and waved his sub-machine-gun. 'The hell with it!' he bawled. 'Let's get them! Wipe out the bastards!'

The men cheered and jumped up and started running across the deck. The guns of the terrorists cut some down, but those left kept on going. Masters found himself near the drilling room, where he heard screams and saw terrorists convulsing as they collapsed and rolled over. A grenade exploded and tore the running men apart; another flew down from the roof of the drilling room to add its deafening explosion to the general bedlam. Glancing up, Masters saw the terrorists firing from the roof. Simultaneously a hail of bullets thudded into the deck behind him and ricocheted off the nearby modules. A grenade exploded above him, searing the gloom with jagged white light; there was screaming and a man somersaulted as he plunged to the deck.

Then Masters saw Hubbert: he was on a ladder, clambering up the side of the drilling room, his weapon dangling from his free hand. Masters followed without thinking, but the corporal's huge frame disappeared above him. Still climbing, Masters felt almost numb from the roaring and shouting. Reaching the roof, he saw a group of armed terrorists crouching around the hole in the drilling shaft. A lot of them fell when the SBS troops fired at them. A few screamed and staggered back against the shaft and plunged down the moonpool.

Masters saw sticks of dynamite piled up around one leg, with the wire from a timing device running behind a module.

'Get down!' he bawled.

He threw himself down, slithered back towards the ladder, grabbed the top rung and tugged himself over the edge of the deck and managed to place his feet on a lower rung, holding his weapon in one hand. His whole head seemed to explode, he saw white light and flames, then he dropped through a deafening cacophony, crushing pressure and fierce heat. The sky above seemed to split, there was a rainfall of debris – scorched nuts and bolts, buckled pieces of metal sheeting, dust and cement – and Masters crawled across the deck on his hands and knees, shook his head, then fell face down. The thunder imprisoned him. He was pummelled and scorched. He shook his head again, heard a ringing in his ears, then blinked repeatedly and glanced sideways. The deck was spinning around him, smoke billowed across the modules, and he rolled on to his back and looked up wide-eyed as the whole derrick fell.

Bent by the explosions, the legs were buckling and breaking apart; the tiered platforms started shrieking and tearing loose, then they plunged down the centre. The roof of the drilling room caved in, men and machinery poured down through it, and black smoke billowed up from a wall of flame to form a great mushroom. Finally, the derrick fell, toppling over to the right, exploding in a mass of wood and steel, then crashing over the main deck. Many men screamed as the massive girders fell, bounced over the deck, smashed through men and modules, then flew off the edge of the deck, to plunge into the sea.

Masters scrambled to his feet, feeling dizzy and unreal. He turned around and picked up his Sterling. Then he saw the blond giant.

Hubbert was crawling towards him. His hair had been burnt off. His face was blistered and his wet suit was in tatters and appeared to be smouldering. He crawled right up to Masters and stared at him with dazed eyes. He raised one limp hand in greeting or farewell, then coughed blood and died.

Masters felt a searing rage. He cursed and looked all around him. He saw the dawn light pouring over the sea – but he did not see McGee. Now he wanted McGee; wanted justice for all the dead. He stepped forward and stumbled over another dead man. He cursed again and walked on.

The air was filled with smoke, guns were firing from all sides, and he heard the clatter of booted feet across the catwalks, along with more shouting and screaming. One terrorist flopped across a railing; another swung his legs up; a third cried out in agony as he fell through the air and thumped on to the deck. Masters just kept walking, his nose filled with smoke and cordite. There was a flash and then he heard the explosion and dropped to the deck. The blast pummelled his body; he felt scorched and suffocated. When the explosion subsided, he climbed to his feet and saw a huge wall of yellow flame. One of the oil tanks had exploded, the oil pouring out on fire, and a man rushed from the blaze, screaming dementedly, beating at his own body. He spun around and fell; his body twitched and then was still. Whether a terrorist or SBS, he was still burning badly as Masters stepped past him and walked to the landing-pad catwalk.

The wall of flame scorched Masters and the smoke almost choked him as he stepped on to the narrow, windy catwalk. The storm had passed on and the huge waves had subsided. Masters gazed down two hundred feet and saw a sea strewn with debris. Dead men were drifting down there, bloated, gradually sinking. Weapons and discarded oxygen cylinders were sinking beside them. Farther out, but drifting in towards the rig, were the empty submersibles.

Masters crossed the catwalk, which sloped up to the landing pad. Hearing the sound of gunfire and shouting, he broke into a trot.

He jumped on to the landing pad and saw a Dragonfly at the far side, sliding along the badly tilting deck towards the edge of the landing pad. McGee was going with it. His right arm was stretched above him. The sleeve of his blue overalls had caught on the door handle and he was being dragged backwards along the deck. McGee was covered in blood and screaming wildly as he struggled. Dalton, looking angry, was walking towards him, taking aim with his Browning.

'You cheated us,' Dalton said clearly. 'You won't do that again.'

The helicopter slid towards the edge, taking the screaming McGee with it. Suddenly, Masters realized what was happening and ran towards Dalton. He was too late. He saw Dalton cocking the hammer. McGee was still being dragged backwards along the deck as Dalton aimed at his head. There was no need to shoot him – he was going over the edge, anyway – but Masters saw the American aiming at McGee and he knew it was vengeance.

'No!' Masters roared.

Dalton spun around. Seeing Masters, he knew that the SBS sergeant had overheard his remark and so aimed the handgun at him instead. Masters didn't stop to think. He fired a short, precise burst from his Sterling. The sub-machine-gun roared and Dalton flung his arms out and staggered back like a drunken man, dropping his own weapon. The helicopter kept sliding, with McGee screaming and kicking, as Dalton collapsed to the deck and made no further movement.

McGee screamed again. His heels were dragging along the deck. The tail of the Dragonfly shot into the air and the nose pointed down towards the sea. The wheels caught on the edge, the helicopter flipped over, and McGee flew up and somersaulted with it and seemed to hang in the air. Then the helicopter fell, disappearing from view. McGee's screaming grew faint, then was cut off abruptly when the helicopter plunged into the sea far below.

Masters walked across the deck and checked that Dalton was dead. He then walked to the edge of the landing pad and looked down at the sea. The water boiled up and bubbled, rushed in circles and formed a whirlpool. The tail of the Dragonfly disappeared and then the swirling sea settled down.

Masters went back to the catwalk and looked across the main deck. The deck was sloping down to the right, but it was no longer sinking. The gunfire had ceased. There were dead men everywhere. A few terrorist prisoners with their hands on their heads were being herded by armed SBS men into a module. The whole deck was strewn with debris and covered in drifting smoke. A wall of flame was rising up from the oil tanks and being fanned by the wind.

Crossing the catwalk, Masters looked down at the sea and saw dead bodies, pieces of equipment and bobbing submersibles. He walked on across the main deck and saw Pancroft coming towards him. The captain had taken off the oxygen cylinders, mask and flippers, though he still wore his wet suit and webbed belts. He grinned, waved and then gave the thumbs up, indicating that the hole in the damaged pontoon leg had been sealed and the rig had been saved.

Masters waved back and then turned to survey the choppy grey sea. He saw a rig in the distance, burning off its waste gas. So close to the horizon, it seemed small, isolated and defenceless.

Captain Pancroft walked up beside Masters and placed a consoling hand on his shoulder. The two men stood there and looked out to sea in silence.

17

Masters and Turner, both wearing British United Oil overalls, stood on a catwalk on Bravo 1 and looked out at the Forties Field. The sea was quite calm, the sky was grey and cloudy as usual, and the distant rigs, scattered along the horizon, seemed fragile and lonesome.

As one they glanced down at the landing pad just beneath them. They heard the roar of the Wessex Mk 3 transport helicopter, watched its rotors spinning, and then saw the armed SBS bodyguards emerging from the nearby module. The guards fanned out across the deck, forming a path to the helicopter, their green berets worn proudly on their heads, weapons at the ready. The Prime Minister emerged soon after, walking between the watchful guards, bent against the strong wind and shivering visibly. His silvery-grey hair was ruffled and he was slightly stooped, clearly weary, but when he reached the helicopter and was standing on the top step, he turned back and waved up at the catwalk. Masters and Turner waved back. The

PM studied them for what seemed like a long time, then he turned away and entered the Wessex.

'He's bloody angry,' Turner said. 'It was our mess and yet it trapped him. He had to give us our reduction in oil tax and he won't like us for it.'

'I'm surprised,' Masters replied. 'I thought he had you by the short and curlies. I thought he could have used this whole mess against you and made you settle for less.'

'It doesn't work that way, Tone. You can't fight the oil companies. With the loss of Eagle 3 and the virtual destruction of Charlie 2, Sir Reginald threw up his hands and said we couldn't go on. The PM was flabbergasted. He couldn't believe what he was hearing. But Sir Reginald just looked him in the eye and pointed out what our losses were. He mentioned the cost of rebuilding the rigs, said how long it would take to do it, suggested that British United couldn't possibly survive all that without a substantial reduction in oil tax. The PM was outraged and said the Chairman was blackmailing him. He said the government couldn't pay for the mistakes of incompetent oil companies. Sir Reginald just smiled at him. It was a hell of a smile. He said that the oil companies couldn't afford to return to drilling if they weren't given a reduction in tax to offset their losses. He also told the PM that if the oil companies stopped drilling, the press would want to know why and then word of the terrorist outrage would be bound to slip out. He then pointed out what that would mean: an international loss of confidence in the North Sea in particular and the UK in general. The PM surrendered – and British United Oil is back in business, bigger than ever.'

Masters smiled and glanced down at the landing pad. The Under-Secretary was entering the Wessex, stooping low at the door. The SBS guards followed him in, moving backwards up the steps, their weapons at the ready. The last guard vanished into the helicopter and the loadmaster slid the door shut.

Masters smiled to himself. Though he was now back as an undercover man on Bravo 1, acting as a tool-pusher – just as other SBS men were on other rigs – he knew that if anyone asked about SBS involvement in the North Sea they would be given an official denial. SBS involvement in the North Sea, though vital and ongoing, retained its top secret classification.

'You were right,' Turner said. 'The man behind the hijack was Dalton. It was him all along. Andy Blackburn phoned through with the proof. He'd questioned some of the people listed in McGee's address book and they confirmed that McGee had been seeing Dalton. They first met in the Middle East, when Dalton was negotiating on behalf of the oil companies and McGee was buying weapons for the IRA. They met later in Paris and it's believed they sealed the agreement there.'

'I don't understand,' Masters said. 'That means one of your overseas backers was behind the whole thing.'

'Correct,' Turner replied. 'It certainly seems that way. We can assume that someone in the conglomerate instigated the whole operation.'

'Why would they do that? It doesn't make sense.'

'Yes, it does, my friend. It certainly does if you think in international terms. The conglomerate must have known that if the British government reduced North Sea oil taxes, all the revenue they were giving to their overseas interests would have been diverted into Britain. The conglomerate knew that it was exorbitant British taxes that had forced the subsidiaries to cut back on drilling and invest their capital in the conglomerate's tax-free havens. It was therefore in their own interests to get rid of the Prime Minister, discredit the British oilfields, and ensure that future British oil revenue continued to be dependent on the conglomerate's tax-free – therefore more lucrative – overseas markets.'

'But it backfired,' Masters said.

'Yes. Because of McGee. They didn't think for a minute that the Irishman would stop short at killing a British Prime Minister. They also forgot that it wasn't in the IRA's own interests to instigate the destruction of North Sea oil revenue. Fanatics or not, the IRA are, in their own bloody way, fighting for an Ireland which, though independent, would still require the benefits of North Sea oil. If McGee hadn't wanted that, if he had assassinated the Prime Minister, the North Sea would now be finished and the UK would be forced to buy from elsewhere. As it stands, by what's almost pure chance we've been given the winning hand.'

They looked down at the landing pad, where the Wessex was ready to take off. Its spinning rotors had created a slipstream that lashed at the roustabouts. The landing pad vibrated, roughnecks pulled the blocks away, and the helicopter roared even louder and lifted awkwardly off the deck. It hovered a few seconds, framed by sea and sky, then swayed a little and began its ascent. It climbed steadily, hovered again above the derricks, then turned away like a huge, crippled bird and flew towards the mainland.

'So,' Masters asked, 'what do we do?'

'We do nothing,' Turner said.

Startled, Masters stared at him. 'What the hell do you mean, Keith? You're not trying to find the men behind Dalton? Is *that* what you're saying?'

'Yes, Tone, that's what I'm saying.' Turner tugged at his beard, ran his fingers through his hair, gazed out across the desolate sea and then shrugged forlornly. 'What can we do? Not a damn thing! Dalton was with the conglomerate for years and he knew lots of powerful men. Which one of them gave the order? Which company stood to gain most? Was it the Americans or the Germans or the French or our Middle Eastern friends? We'll never find out. The conglomerate's too big to investigate. Like most of the conglomerates, it's a multinational affair, divorced from any single jurisdiction and removed from morality. And what if we mentioned Dalton? Or accused the conglomerate in general? We'd just receive a faultlessly worded missive denying all knowledge of Dalton's political, financial or criminal activities. They've got us whipped, Tone. There's not a thing we can do about it. We'll just have to get on with our jobs and forget that this ever happened. There's no evidence for their guilt, no authority that can find the truth. The politicians no longer rule the world – the multinationals do.'

Masters sighed, glanced up at the cloudy sky and saw the Wessex, a tiny speck in the distance, flying over another rig before disappearing beyond the horizon as if it had never been.

It's been like a dream, he thought. It might never have happened. Twenty-four hours have passed and apart from the many men dead and wounded, nothing has changed.

Sergeant Masters, SBS, sighed again as he gazed across the sea to the distant horizon. 'Well,' he said, 'at least for the moment Britain still has its oil.'

'Thanks to the SBS,' Turner replied. 'Let's hope it stays that way.'

PRESS RELEASE BRITISH UNITED OIL
DATE: 20 August 1982

UNCLASSIFIED

1. On 18 August 1982, at approximately 1830 hours, an earth tremor travelling from north to south along the bed of the North Sea caused extensive damage to some of British United Oil's major oilfields. Shock waves from the tremor caused extreme turbulence on the sea's surface with winds of approximately 150 miles per hour and waves as high as 120 feet. As a result, Eagle 3, the main semi-submersible rig on the Frigg Field, was sunk with all hands. The tremor then travelled on a south-westerly course until it reached the Beryl Field where, before dissipating, it caused considerable damage to the main rig, Charlie 2, and led to the unfortunate deaths of twenty crew members who were trapped beneath a collapsed section of the drilling floor.

2. As Eagle 3 (Frigg Field) was being prepared for

shut-down and towing to another site, no plans for its reconstruction are envisaged.

3. Charlie 2 (Beryl Field) has been shut down temporarily for extensive repairs and the surviving crew members repatriated for medical examination and subsequent transfer to other rigs.

4. As many of the crew members are suffering from severe trauma it is felt by this Company that their names should be withheld from the media and general public. Private settlement of compensation for the dependants of the deceased is currently being negotiated.

5. A full investigation into the nature of the earth tremor has been ordered and a complete, top-classified report will be submitted in due course to the Under-Secretary of the Department of Energy. For reasons of internal security British United Oil has agreed with the Department of Energy that no further information regarding this matter should be released.

continued overleaf . . .